UNBREAKABLE

J. B. James

Published by J. B. James
Hardback ISBN13: 978-1-7356645-0-7
Paperback ISBN13: 978-1-7356645-1-4
Electronic ISBN13: 978-1-7356645-2-1

To my wife Ashlynn, thank you for getting me back into reading.
To my daughters Zcearia and Zania, thank you for your love and allowing me to be your dad.
And lastly, to my parents, William and Doris, thank you for everything.

TERENCE CRUTCHER, PHILANDO CASTILE, SAMUEL DUBOSE, MICHAEL BROWN, FREDDIE GRAY, TAMIR RICE, WALTER SCOTT, ALTON STERLING, JAMAR CLARK, JEREMY McDOLE, ERIC HARRIS, ERIC GARNER, AHMAUD ARBERY, BREONA TAYLOR, GEORGE FLOYD, AND THE GROWING LIST OF BROWN-SKINNED AMERICANS KILLED AT THE HANDS OF SOCIAL INJUSTICE.

UNBREAKABLE

BOOK ONE OF THE UPPER LIMIT SERIES

ONE

Narrock

Narrock's muscles tensed as the training field went silent. Even the world of Jhatar seemed to hold her breath when the clouds gave way and the full attention of the sun settled upon this battle. Sweat beaded upon Narrock's face as he tightened his grip on his twin-axe heritage. Across from him, five adepts taunted him. The oldest of all the warrior trainees, Bhurron, was massive. He stood a full length taller than the rest of the males, his onyx skin and ash-covered back terrified all the other trainees, but not Narrock.

"Are you sure about this?" an instructor asked.

He just nodded his head. Sparring sessions usually were one-on-one contests, but today's exhibition was different. Narrock turned a blind eye to the insults about his brother. *The hell if I care*, would have been his response, but when they disrespected his father he responded with a challenge.

"Just remember. You asked for this," Bhurron said. The earth shook as his giant iron-spiked heritage thudded against it, his bronze eyes locked against Narrock's amber stare.

"I will make you eat your words."

At the signal to begin, Narrock released his senses and extended his perception three times the length of his body in every direction. His father, a legend among the elite fighters known as the Gwhin, taught him the importance of the first strike. Fast as lightning, He slammed the blunt side of his heritage into Korbin's exposed neck. His body had not even collapsed to the floor before he had engaged with A'nark. The blur of his deep sienna flesh against the yellow tint of A'nark's skin filled the air. A brawler, A'nark wielded duel golden-knuckle heritages allowing him to fight effectively in close-quarter combat. Before A'nark's heritage could catch his iron-forged chin, he spun around as another one of Bhurron's cronies attempted to attack him from behind. The sound of A'nark's fist connecting with the other boy's face was muffled by the crunch of Narrock embedding the back-side of his axes into A'nark's thick skull. His knees faltered, and Narrock kicked him into the path of the charging Jerren.

At that moment, Narrock dared a look in Bhurron's direction.

He had not moved since the exhibition started. Grinding his teeth, he holstered his heritages. He decided he would finish this fight barehanded and deliver this prick the beating he deserved. Without even looking, Narrock deflected Jerren's attack. Of the five boys, only Jerren's terracotta flesh was inked. The story of the sly fox forever immortalized on his—it was too late. Foolishly scanning the tale on his arm, he did not shut his eyes in time. Fire radiated through his optical nerves, and despite his urgent commands, his eyes refused to open or stop watering. Bhurron's laughter cut through his pain. Narrock found his blistering hot fingers drifting for the familiar assurance of his heritage, but stopped short of releasing them from their sleep. He reminded himself that he did not need them or his sight for this. Calming his breathing, he extended his perception once more, and took a fighter's position. He waited. He sensed the two boys circling him while Bhurron had yet to move.

In unison, the two boys attacked. Baring his teeth, he felt his flesh constrict and morph into an impenetrable defense. In this state, the damage he received was easily nullified. He deflected their heritages and withstood their attacks as if they were nothing. Even though they were his seniors by two cycles, his ten life cycles had been better spent under the tutelage of his father and brother. The fact that he released his emotional limits and achieved hardening of this magnitude while they had not was proof. As his eyes cleared, Narrock slammed an elbow into Jerren's sternum before launching his fist into his second opponent.

The satisfying sounds of crunching bones, accentuated by limp bodies hitting the ground, brought a slight curl to his lips.

The sound of flesh on flesh sliced the air as Bhurron mocked his appreciation of Narrock's skill. Breathing raggedly, Narrock turned in his direction. As he walked through the carnage, intentionally stepping over each body, he unhooked his heritage and allowed them to fall to the ground. The sign was clear.

"Who do you think you are?" Bhurron asked, his knuckles turning white as his grip sank into his heritage.

Narrock said nothing. Each step he took saw Bhurron's face shift from amusement to anger. It did not bother him that his challenge would go unanswered as Bhurron picked up his heritage. The embers in his eyes burst into a wildfire as he pounced.

All six warriors woke in the healing hall. Pressing against the unforgiving surface to rest on his elbows, Narrock cautiously eyed Bhurron sitting on the bed across from him before sitting up straight. From the looks of things, he could tell he beat the hell out of him. However, the tender patches across his body and his swollen eye meant he'd also taken a beating. The two males stared at each other for a moment before breaking the silence.

"I'm sorry," Bhurron said, his swollen face. "I won't say

why I did it, but I will say you're one tough bastard. You have my respect."

Narrock's brow furrowed. He never heard Bhurron apologize to anyone, not even the masters. Still, he felt as if he somehow, after exchanging fists and leaving each other bloodied and bruised, understood him better. Even though he did not speak, Narrock nodded his head as a silent message passed between two equals. They both looked at each other a moment longer before they found themselves drifting back into sleep.

TWO

Rogue Traders

" Sir, we cannot sustain our course if we don't stop and restock our inventory."

Dro knew his supply chief was correct, yet he did not feel comfortable stopping. It had been nearly a month since Dro, a former Routen commander for the Reinzour, executed a failed coup d'é·tat and subsequent fleeing. It was not that he was someone who did not care for the Valencian people. He just thought he deserved what the Reinzour had. In his utter defeat, he went from living a luxurious and lavish life to being hunted like every other beast.

"The supplies won't matter if those damn blow-hard

commanders find us."

Dro thought he understood the depths of the Reinzour's power, but now with his life on the line, he was regretting his decision. The Reinzour was the ruler of Ryzanu and leader of twenty-four Routen. A direct descendant of the Supreme Ruler, his prowess was far beyond anything Dro could understand. It was only by some miracle he escaped with his life. Now he only wished to preserve it. The sleepless nights were taking their toll, and he spent every moment looking over his shoulder. Despite his faithful soldiers, he did not give a damn about their lives. They were simply pawns for him to discard at his leisure and when he reached his safe haven, a secret world he made sure no one knew about, he would decide then if they would continue to live. All of a sudden the ship was in chaos. Sirens reverberated up and down the cabins along with screams and unsecured objects slamming against the walls.

"Sir, we aren't sure how, but the ship has been caught in some kind of pull."

Placing his meaty fingers around the soldier's throat. "If you don't get us the bloody hell out of here, I will burn the flesh from your face and FEED IT TO YOUR DAMN CHILDREN!"

The soldier quickly retreated and started barking orders like a mad man. Dro maneuvered his way to the front of the ship, "What the bloody hell is that?!" He stared in horror as the ship became completely quiet. They all stared at what looked like space falling in on itself taking all types of exotic matter with it. "GET US THE HELL OUT OF HERE!", but it was too late. Just as he bellowed his command—the ship was swallowed.

Passing through the folds of space, the crew was bombarded with flashes of bright lights and the full spectrum of every color they could imagine and then some. And just like that, the ship was released on the other side of space itself. The soldiers' thunderous celebration was cut short as Dro's behemoth-like voice boomed through the cheers.

"Someone tell me why the hell my ship smells like piss and shit?!"

He demanded the pilots find a place to land. Passing through space was disorienting and now his ship smelt like an over-sized septic tank. He had to get some fresh air.

"Sir, where are we?"

Dro and his crew traveled throughout the cosmos hundreds of times, but this was a region he had never seen. Engaging the ships cloaking system, the pilot carefully entered Jhatar's atmosphere and landed in a clearing guarded heavily by trees which provided excellent coverage. Not bothering to scan the atmospherics of Jhatar, Dro burst out of the ship and demanded the aircraft be cleaned.

"If I smell even the slightest hint of shit on this plane, I will leave you on this damned planet to rot."

He did not wait around to see his order complete. Instead, he ventured out to survey the immediate area. Luckily for him, the planet seemed habitable.

Three sun cycles passed, and Narrock was finally feeling like himself again. When he returned to the training fields following his infamous match, he received acknowledging nods from the masters.

"It is good to see you are well, young Narrock. Your father would be proud."Master Centrine's voice was like honey.

The weight of her hand against his shoulder provided silent comfort for him. Of the masters preparing the students for the temple of Rhundumah—the release of the physical limits— she was the only one to have known and fought alongside his father. And she had been there the day he was killed.

Swallowing a lump in his throat, he forced back the emotions stored in his heart. "Thank you," he said bowing deeply before excusing himself.

No sooner than he left her side was he approached by

Bhurron, A'nark, Jerren, and two other boys. Narrock clenched his fists and prepared himself for what was next.

"Bro, chill. It isn't even like that," Bhurron exposed his palms and slightly dipped his head.

Bhurron picked up where he left off in the healing halls. Out of the corner of his eye, Narrock watched as Allister approached them. Although he was fascinated by her ivory hair interspersed with flecks of plum strands, he never paid her any real attention. Now, though, something about the way she moved in his direction made him tune out Bhurron and focus solely on her. It was almost as if her body was moving aimlessly and she was absentminded. Just as she reached him, she began spouting off towards Bhurron in defense of Narrock.

Narrock looked at her in bewilderment. This runt, his junior, was tearing into Bhurron and the other adepts with such visceral hatred that he found himself smiling at the looks on their faces. Returning his gaze to the small figure with the boisterous mouth, he watched as she blushed, and her eyes widened when she realized everyone was now staring at her.

"Look, Narrock's got a bodyguard," A'nark snickered.

Narrock's eyes snapped to him, and satisfaction rushed over him when the older male lowered his gaze and took a submissive step back. His eyes once again returned to the girl as he raised a brow trying to understand why she felt it necessary to stick her neck into affairs that had nothing to do with her. Lost in the bizarreness of the spiraling situation, he had not taken notice of Jerren positioning himself behind her. With a quick extension of his hands into her back, Allister flailed through the air, desperately trying to grab onto something only to awkwardly land in Narrock's arms.

"Hey man, we were just having a little fun. We only came to tell you, you know, you're alright with us." Bhurron did nothing to hide the smirk on his face at the sight of the girl draped over his arm. "Anyways, we'll leave you two alone," his grin widened as he placed his hands behind his head, gingerly walking away.

Narrock stared at the girl still lying awkwardly in his arms. He found himself looking at his own reflection in her deep blue eyes infused with silver. He was keenly aware of her boney frame pressed against his and the stupid look on her face—like she was having a seizure. Then, he abruptly dropped her to the ground and walked to where the masters were calling.

"Before you can master your upper limits, you must first master your inner limits." Master Centrine's voice commanded the attention of every warrior on the training grounds. "It is not enough to harness the gift if you are too weak to control its power. The time has come for us to gauge your level of mastery of the fundamental elements of your training."

"Sight, smell, hearing, taste, and touch," the hearty baritone voice of Master Shrett picked up, "these are the lights that guide us to live, fight, and grow. And they are also the darkness which hides us from our enemies. As such, each of you will embrace the darkness as a pack. If you can remain uncaptured until morning light, you will have passed this test."

"We're playing Seek and Conceal?" Allister asked.

Narrock rolled his eyes. While he did not have an unfavorable opinion of her, he often found her quite dense.

"As stated before, before you can master your upper limits, you must master the fundamentals," Master Shrett said.

As excitement filled the camp at the idea of playing a game for training, Narrock's eyes darted from the three masters to the hoard of trainees. When his eyes met Master Centrine's he asked, "Who are we concealing from?"

And with a sick sadist smile, Master Verris whispered, "That is a good question if you didn't already know the answer."

"Sir, there are ten foreign children just south of us."

"Please explain to me why I care?" Dro asked.

"Sir, I've never seen people like them, and I was just

thinking maybe—"

"That is where you went wrong, I never asked you to think. What the hell do I care about a few foreign mongrels?" Turning his attention to the ground commander, "Are we finally ready to get off this damned planet?"

It had been several days since they landed here after passing through what could only be described as the insides of space and Dro could not shake the fact the Reinzour might catch up to him.

"Sir, we should be ready to leave as soon as the sun recedes."

Narrock walked behind the group, silently cursing himself for being stuck with Bhurron and his idiots, as well as Allister. He could tell she was still embarrassed by the way she trudged in front of everyone. Everything about her body language spoke to her undisciplined nature. He never did understand why Master Centrine had spent so much time on a wasted talent like her.

Just then, Narrock and several others perceived something was wrong. He saw them and cursed as Allister, oblivious to everything, continued wallowing in her emotions. Riding the wind, he grabbed her and slung her to the ground, covering her mouth with his hand. As she struggled to free herself, his grip became firm until she bit him.

"Get off!" She pushed his chest from hers, but he had her straddled between his legs. "First you're holding me, then you decide to drop me on the floor, and now you're tackling me—"

"Would you shut up," A'nark said. Motioning with his finger, he pointed to where Dro and his crew were.

"I've never seen an iron box like that. What do you think it is for?" Jerren asked.

Narrock signaled for everyone to retreat. "They don't appear to know we are here. We need to find Master Centrine and tell her what we've seen."

He silently peeled his body from Allister's and they began to slowly return to the training fields careful not to notify the possible threat of their existence. Destiny had other plans as loose footing sent Bhurron tumbling down the hillside taking Allister with him and exposing their location.

In an instant, Narrock and the others were down the hill assuming defensive positions for Bhurron and Allister to recover. Being of a stocky build, Bhurron took the fall with only a few scratches, but Allister cried in agony when she was unable to put any weight on her left leg. Narrock surveyed the bone protruding from her leg, the sight of her inner flesh on full display. His prayers she would not notice were quickly dashed as his ear was shattered by the high-pitched scream he heard next.

Dro's upper lip raised and revealed a bastard's smile. "What do we have here?"

His eyes scanned the ten children in their fighting positions. His soldiers made quick work of the children, and everyone froze when they heard the forest ruffling. The tree-line gave way to an elderly female. She locked her stare on him as his soldiers formed a protective wall. Dro forced his way through his men, his eyes connecting with the Master's and then passed to where only Narrock stood. He cocked his head when he noticed one of his soldiers lying lifeless on the ground, an axe firmly wedged atop his skull.

"Sir, these are the kids I was telling you about."

"I didn't ask, so shut the hell up." Turning his attention back to the female, "And who the hell are you?" he asked, cautiously eying her while remaining aware of Narrock's position.

He watched as she flicked her ears almost as if she was trying to understand. Irritation marred his face as her response seemed to be nothing more than a jumble of unrecognizable

21

syllables and sounds. He watched her eyes constantly dart from him to the pile of limp bodies on the ground, save for the brown boy, and laughed as he watched them attempt to huddle together behind the boy for protection.

"Are you mad we beat the shit out of your brats?"

Then it felt as if she was speaking to the male child, her face tilted in his direction, but she never removed her stare from him. Dro, puzzled by whatever it was the female said, only laughed as the male child eased his stance. In a flash, Dro grabbed the dagger at his side and launched it right through Narrock's shoulder.

Dro snickered when the female charged into action. He watched in awe as the female made quick work of the soldiers attempting to protect him. Her body seized and her eyes darted in every direction as his soldiers began releasing their magic. The corners of his lips touched both his ears and the ground rose in chunks while they fired stones straight at her. She could not overcome them.

Dro waited until his soldiers rendered the female destitute before stepping to the front. Letting out a vile laugh, he grabbed the woman from the ground by her face and waited. He waited as those ten sets of eyes found their way to his victim. He reveled watching despair squeeze the life out of their ugly faces. Flashing a sinister smile, he commanded fire to engulf his hand and laughed until the flesh melted from the old woman's face.

THREE

Hailey and Veronica

It had been ten years since Allister watched Master Centrine's face melt, pooled at her feet as her body disintegrated into ash. She had been haunted by nightmares ever since. So much happened that she often found herself wishing for the peaceful slumber of death. *Anything was better than this*, she thought to herself. As if watching her Master die was not hard enough, Allister and her kindred were taken captive. They were ripped from their home on Jhatar, experienced the brief terror and excitement that came with passing through a kaleidoscope of colors, only to emerge in the abyss of darkness and have their ship invaded. The intruders again, forced them to watch the slaughtering of every soldier on board. At first, she believed it was a miracle that they were found in this rescue mission, but every day since waking up in this hell-hole, her mind often wished she had been among those slaughtered.

"Alli, it's not in the easy times when you find out who you are, but it's the trying times that will reveal the truth of your character." She felt that familiar warmth press the top of her head. "With each trying time, you must decide who you want to be."

Tears flowed from her eyes at remembering the words of her master. It was only by her words she managed to make it this long.

"I will not forget who I am, or where I have come from."

She wiped the tears from her face as she stood tall speaking to her own reflection. When they arrived on Ryzanu, they were stripped of everything. Forced to learn a new language and sold to the highest bidder. Well, the girls anyways. Before Mautivia could be sold, she attacked a guard and was beheaded right in front of everyone—a warning resistance would not be tolerated. But the worst part—as if her horror-frozen head landing at Alli's feet was not bad enough—she, along with everyone else, had been stripped of her own name.

"Hailey, do you intend to skip your duties today?"Brista

asked.

Brista was responsible for the daily preparations at the Ishtar house. The Reinzour's Routen were made up of twenty-four houses where the heads made up his elite commanders who reigned over thousands of Toultyn. Isthar was one of the Routen, and as Alli was his slave, her responsibility was to feed his men and care for his house.

"I will be right there," Alli said, still not acknowledging this name she was given.

Quickly, she donned her clothes and rushed down the hallway. There had been one good thing to happen to her since arriving on this awful world. She at least had the comfort of being enslaved with the one person who understood her the most.

"Alli, could you at least try not to get on her bad side, you're going to get yourself killed one of these days," Ionis said in their native tongue.

"These are not my kings, and I have no intention of rolling over and letting them think so."

While she talked a big game, she knew the truth. Deep down inside, she was a coward. The only reason she could even speak so defiantly was because only Ionis understood their native tongue. This became their pitiful attempt to remember they were Jazwon Warriors.

"Veronica, you're needed. Go clean the halls now," Brista said.

Ionis' eyes somersaulted beneath her eye lids. "Well, I guess that's me."

"Same place then?"

"After they almost caught us last time?"

"Veronica!" Brista said, losing her patience.

"Look, find a spot and let me know. I have a feeling I'm going to need to punch something to keep from punching her."

FOUR

That is Not My Name

"Get out of my way, boy," the head guard said.

Narrock, fixing his eyes on Ba'al, "My name is not boy."

"Your name is whatever I decide. Now, get out of my way." Narrock only squared his shoulders and set his feet. "I said move."

Narrock flared his nostrils and sneered as he looked down on the guard who was at least half a foot taller. The guard began to reach down into the depths of that strange power they had when Bhurron, A'nark, and Jerren flanked his side. Together, they had been called the Four Dragons. At least, that is what the other fighters called them. Of the hundreds of enslaved fighters, they managed to hold onto their identities from before their lives were ripped away to become subservient nothings. Narrock smirked when Ba'al released the shards of iron orbiting his hands.

"Derrius, your life is worth more than your pride," Kazwe said.

Narrock most loathed Kazwe and his unofficial standing as leader among the imprisoned. Yielding, he stepped aside and allowed the guard to pass.

"You will learn your place, boy," Ba'al slammed his shoulder and grunted at Narrock's solidity before finally pushing his way by.

"Must you always antagonize the guard, Derrius?"

Ignoring Kazwe, the Four Dragons turned to return to training when he felt Kazwe's dirty nails dig into his shoulder.

"Derrius, you're playing a dangerous—"

"If you continue to address me by that name, you will find out just how dangerous I play."

When they arrived, seven of Narrock's kindred found themselves in the Coliseum. Today, only Narrock, Bhurron, A'nark, and Jerren remained. In an attempt to break the will of the group two were killed upon arrival to Ryzanu. The death of his other kindred came during the challenge. The Reinzour's mistake was believing since some of the male children were capable fighters, all of them were. His death came quickly when his opponent's fist ripped through his chest and wrapped around his heart while his ears were filled with the sound of laughter. Then in one fluid motion, he clutched his heart in his hand, and it exploded.

"If they say your name is Derrius, then you gutter-swiving name is Derrius." In an instant, he was across the room.

"I will never accept a name that was not meant for me. I am not like you. I will not allow these visceral cockroaches to steal from me who I am. I am Narrock, and it will do you well to remember it." Everyone was now watching the exchange.

Snarling, Kazwe settled himself and asked. "Whether it's Derrius or Narrock, what does it matter if you're dead?"

Before he could answer, Bhurron spoke.

"Because, when we are dead, the legends will tell of the sons of Jhatar, the ones who refused to bow."

FIVE

Tribute

Walking down the corridor leading to the Routen's study, Alli's palms were sweating and her eyes darted in every direction. The passage was filled with all kinds of trinkets and a valuable painting of the cosmos in which she existed. She screamed as her legs gave way. Encased before her was the severed head of some sea creature spiked atop a trident. At first, she thought she imagined it staring down at her, but then it blinked and she found herself on all fours scrambling to get away from it.

She gathered the Routen led massive exploration teams to search the furthest reaches of the stars. Every time they returned with gems, minerals, and all kinds of exotic weaponry and technology. But, never had Alli seen something like that. Then she felt the familiar pangs in her chest as her thoughts drifted to not just her people, but all the different creeds of people enslaved around the house. She shuttered and continued down the corridor, filing this information away.

Since she started serving in the Routen's house, Alli had been secretly conducting her own reconnaissance. She took advantage of the Toultyn who consistently failed to hold their liquor. She marveled at how much they were willing to spill after only a few mugs of cider. Gleaning any information from the Routen's Shadows was difficult. These were the ranking members of his court. From the information she gathered and managed to piece together, she learned that this was not their home. Initially anyway, before they ransacked this place and stolen the land away from its people, it seemed very few of the indigenous people were still alive. From time to time, she would catch a glimpse of them, they were something of a consort to the Reinzour, but the majority of the survivors were trapped in the voids. However, the best intelligence came from the stories of their expeditions, and for Alli, the hope of one day leaving this place and returning home. There was one thing she had yet to figure out. Where did all the males go?

"Alli!" a voice echoed from behind, and she whirled

around in delight.

"Ionis, what are you doing here?" she embraced her kindred before holding her at arm's length.

"How should I know, the guard came and told me Routen Ishtar wanted to see me."

Just then the large mahogany doors swung open to Ishtar's private study, and they were ushered in.

"Sit here," the guardsman commanded before taking his spot on the wall.

Alli's jaw dropped, and her breathing stopped. This had to be the most beautiful room she had ever seen. The intricately carved bookshelves scaled to the ceiling. Alli could read the stories etched into the polished wood. She cast a glance over to Ionis, who could not take her eyes off the colossal chandelier dangling in the middle of the study. The light poured in from the skylights, positioned in a way that emphasized each crystal dancing in the sun as it glided across the sky. It was all so lovely, and just as their enchantment by the room peaked, their souls plummeted back into their bodies at the sound of the husky, seductive voice of Routen Ishtar.

"It is not often many females see this room, but you can imagine what happens when they do."

Alli and Ionis straightened in their seats redirecting their gaze to the head of the house. In the seven years they had been in this house, they rarely saw the Routen. Usually, he was tended to by his hand-picked Valencian fancies. He was beautiful. Alli could not help but notice how light seemed to emanate from his pale skin. She took in his short, jet black hair curling around his ears, and his exposed dimples graciously ebbed in unison with his lips. *His lips...*, she began wondering how his plush lips would feel pressed against hers. For him to take her in slowly and appraise every inch of her the way she found herself doing to him.

"I take it you like what you see," he said with a smirk. Alli blushed, and Ionis gave her a look that said she was not alone. "I am told you two are under Brista's care and have been my servants for seven years now?" He admired the curves of each girl, but his eyes lingered when they met Alli's. "What I'm curious to know is, how do you like it here?"

Alli looked to Ionis, who looked right back at her. A silent request for her to answer.

"We are happy to be in your care."

The learning halls drilled into the females to always provide a quick and short answer when speaking to authority.

"Come now, you needn't be so formal. Please, please, relax."

Unsure of how to oblige, both girls released the tension in their shoulders and allowed a small bow to sneak into their spine.

"How old were you before you came here?"

Thinking back, Allie was only nine birth cycles or years as they called it, and Ionis was slightly older than her. At that moment it dawned on her, she did not know exactly when her birth was. She knew they were at least nineteen years old, but was not exactly sure when it happened.

"Nine, sir." The honorific felt strange on her tongue. *He couldn't be more than twenty-five himself*, she thought.

"One of the missions of the Routen is to explore the cosmos to collect different exotics, return here to Ryzanu, and report our findings back to the Reinzour." Alli already knew this through her own investigating. "For decades, we have traveled and seen the mysterious, as well as the unexplainable; however, the explanation I find most elusive is where exactly that bastard Dro found you and the males."

Her heart froze. She had never been able to find anything regarding Narrock or the others, but now she might finally learn something. She fought to suppress the hope welling up inside her.

"Are you saying they are still alive?"

35

Just as the words left her mouth, she was surprised to feel a warm liquid flow down her chin, along with the odd taste of salt mixed with metal. It was not until the room stopped spinning that she realized what happened.

"You do not question Routen Ishtar, you whore." The guardsman erected his posture and took his place back on the wall.

Ishtar allowed his eyes to slowly return to the females sitting before him. "You must have forgotten. You have no place to question me."

The implied threat was clear. This had been a warning, and yet, for some reason, Alli's skin tingled as heat pulsated from areas of her body she could not understand.

"My question is still in need of an answer."

At this, she was reminded of something her master once told her, *The danger of an ambush is not catching your prey off-guard, it's making them so intoxicated with the flower that they willingly ignore the thorns.*

She faced him. "We are unsure. On our world we were training and then," choking back the emotions clawing at her throat, "Dro killed our Master. Everything after that is not clear, not until we arrived here." she answered his question without sharing everything.

"So he killed your Master, and then, out of *nowhere*, his ship appears, and you don't know how you ended up in the middle of space?"

"We do not have metal birds—"

"Ships. They are called ships."

"We don't have ships and didn't understand what was going on," her hands restless in her lap. "We are taught how to survive, and at the time, survival meant to be quiet and do as we were told."

The way the Routen questioned her triggered her to recall the interrogation training her Master put her through. She could hear Master Centrine repeat her herself every time she failed.

"Truths and facts are not the same. The truth is nothing more than what is perceived as real, while facts are indisputable. Lies interlaced with facts are how you survive."

She could not grasp the situation entirely, but her gut was screaming at her that if too much was revealed, her people would be in danger.

"What is your name?"

She noticed the change in his posture as he leaned forward, his chin now resting on his hands.

"Hailey—"

"I asked, what is your name?" every word clipped and intentional.

She involuntarily stiffened her shoulders and sat up straight. "Allister."

She watched as his face contracted, head slightly tilted to the side as he pondered her name before he turned to Ionis.

"Ionis." her voice cracked as her name was caught in her throat.

Feigning disinterest, he leaned back in his seat and thunked his feet on the polished redwood desk before him. "The Reinzour is having a tournament, and I want to know more about the males who came with you when we found you." The muscles in Alli's jaw started working when the image of Ionis, head cocked sideways, snapped her mouth shut. "Four males remain from your world," he paused and waited for the information to register. "After we killed three, with little effort mind you, it was assumed the males from your planet had no value. Yet, these four have made quite a name for themselves."

Rising from his seat, he casually strolled to the front of his desk where he crossed his arms and legs and rested against the solid wood.

Alli's heart threatened to burst through her chest. *They're alive*! Her thoughts an ecstasy of relief, but she remained steeled on the outside.

"What I want to know is, should I choose one of them as my representative?"

Alli exchanged looks with Ionis. If they answered yes and were wrong, it would certainly mean death. But if they said no, when would they ever have a chance to see them again? The weight of the question weighed heavily upon them.

"We would first need to see them, and maybe see the other fighters, if possible," Ionis said. The pressure of his gaze was unbearable, and unable to withstand it, their chins reached for their chest for comfort.

"For what purpose?"

Allister's eyes darting from the floor to Ishtar, and back again, "It's been ten years since we last saw them, and I'm not willing to bet my life on a memory."

Ishtar recognized the truth in her answer, and he had not realized the possibility that his intention to play the females could back-fire. At least not until the flesh, bitten by his nails, spoke through rivulets of blood of how he played himself.

SIX

Debrief

"Seems they're not as dumb as you thought," a figure said, emerging from the dark.

"It would appear that way." Ishtar stared at the now closed door. "Report."

The figure materialized from the shadows and took a seated position in the chair now vacated by the servants. "Well, for starters, it would appear the four of them have not taken a liking to our ways."

"You're wasting my time."

"Well, among the slaves, they are referred to as 'the Four

Dragons.' Although I feel the winged fighters would be better deserving that title. At least until they broke their wings." He raised an eyebrow. "Oh, it was to protect the guards. Apparently, they believed they could just chain the poor bastards, but after one guard's skull was crushed in a diving head slam, and another impaled in several vital areas, better judgment prevailed."

"Are they strong?"

"Not particularly. They're extremely fast and agile, but strength, not so much. Now, if you are talking strength, there is another group of fighters that's been segregated from the rest and is said to be the most dangerous of them all."

"And what do you make of them?" he asked, taking his seat behind his desk.

After a moment's thought, the figure spoke. "I do not think these fighters are capable of following. It seems they are more damaged goods than willing recruits."

Throwing himself back in his chair, he sighed deeply as he began drumming his fingers. "What good news, if any, have you brought?"

He knew his position among the Routen was at stake. Every successful tournament meant increasing the strength and status of his house with the Reinzour. He managed to raise the reputation of his house significantly over the last ten years as one of only three Routen to have multiple wins in that period. With a third victory, he was sure to be able to fill the vacancy left by Dro after his failed coup. Dro's house held the supreme spot among the Routen and was the Reinzour's Second House. It was this title Ishtar was desperate to claim.

"Well, if you must know, there does seem to be something different about the four dragons you were curious about."

This caught his attention enough to regain his composure. Again he focused his attention on the cloaked figure.

"As I have stated, they haven't taken a liking to our customs. They are brutal fighters, but they don't fight to maim or kill like the others. It's as if they have no equal and they view their matches as sparring bouts. They fear no one. Not the guards, the fighters, or the Toultyn. But, what is most interesting is that they are the only ones who refuse the names we gave them."

Ishtar massaged his scowling face then worked his way through his hair before slamming his fist on his desk. The figure did not flinch.

"Why is this even important?"

He watched as the hood was pulled back freeing phoenix fire hair as she let out an amused laughed. "Because it says they have no equal." She stood and poured herself a drink.

"Think about it, why don't we bother asking them their names when they come here? Instead, we tell them who they are?" she paused. "Because if we let them have their names it gives them hope. It tells them there is some possibility we are not as supreme as we are. It gives them strength to one day rebel against us. We strip them of their name, their culture, and all of their individuality so we can rule them, control them. These four are the only ones who refuse to be broken." She placed her palms flat on the desk and willed him to try to break her gaze. "Win their trust, and you inherit their strength."

Small depressions appeared on his cheeks as understanding grasped him. "And how do you suppose we go about that?"

SEVEN

The Den

It had been weeks since Alli and Ionis were summoned, and neither of them heard from nor were seen by the Routen. Alli spent her days as usual. Slave girl by day, warrior training with Ionis by night. Although lately, there was a little more motivation. Each night, they meditated on their Masters' words as they worked to improve their upper abilities.

Today, Alli was sent to run an errand at the edge of Ishtar's territory. There were similarities between the city and her home-world. There the landscape was covered with greenery. Trees resembled giant ladders into the celestial thrones, with foliage spanning various vibrant hues. Bodies of electric blue waters transparent as crystal. Every village in constant celebration at the birth of the next generation, the intertwining of souls in unity, and even at the passing of spirits from this world to the next. Life was vivacious, and communion was life. Here, while it was not as vibrant, many of the same could be found. The people walking down paved streets littered with shops on every side, the scent of fresh breads and pastry filling the air. Women adorned in elaborate fabrics and jewels walking with their children. Some power they called electricity, lighting every store and home. These people lived like gods. However, that was not true in this part of Ishtar's lands. These ghettos housed cutthroat merchants ready to swindle every rennie off you. It was a cesspool of orgies and debauchery, full of low-lives and those unable to wield the elements.

Entering the outer region of the town square, Alli jumped back narrowly avoiding the putrid stream of piss as a young boy drew spirals on the wall separating the town from the inner city.

"Stop that, before the Watchers catch you," snapped a woman whom she assumed was the child's mother.

The boy, aware of her gaze, turned sideways and grinned before making a vulgar gesture and running off. She shuddered, trying to erase the image from her mind. She learned years ago to never stay in one place for very long, so she continued on her errand as if she had seen nothing.

45

Reaching into her pocket, she felt for the warn crumpled-up parchment. Though she had been sent to the city before, this town was new to her. Unfolding the parchment, she rotated the make-shift map, attempting to ascertain her location. Alli's ears twitched when shouts and cheering caught her attention. She took another glance at the map. Realizing this was her destination. Reasoning that it would not cause her any trouble, she allowed herself a moment to give in to her curiosity and followed the sounds.

Two days ago, when Alli returned to her room, she found the map along with a request from Ishtar to come to this location to retrieve a package. Before leaving, she tried to gather information on who she was supposed to meet, a name or description—anything really—but her efforts were of little avail. So she shrugged her shoulder and assumed the mysterious delivery person would recognize her.

Pushing back the cumbersome tent flaps, Alli was overwhelmed by the scent of unwashed bodies mixed with blood. The eruption of cheers dulled her sense of smell, and every bone in her body reverberated. Her head on a constant swivel, she took in the onlookers. She watched gamblers wage rennie, then her eyes fell upon the giant metal cage sitting at the heart of the sea of spectators, and her entire body went taut. Wanting to get a better view, she stacked crates to act as a platform and what she saw stole her breath. Inside the cage, she saw two women battling. Her eyes widened as the hairier female held a strong guard against the taller one's barrage of punches. Alli saw the attack before it happened and wondered why the hairy one did not. As the taller woman shifted her weight and landed a hard blow against her opponent's abdomen. Her guard broken, the tall one did not move to land a finishing punch, but instead locked her hands around the back of her opponent's neck and drove her knee through the woman's face. Alli covered her eyes. She heard the crunch of bone and was horrified by the hairy fighter's nose flowing like a faucet, but she could not stop herself from peering through her fingers.

The bloodied woman staggered back a few paces before regathering herself. Her scream sliced through the air and Alli cringed as the woman charged. Leaping into the air, the blood from her nose resembled a floating river, as she placed all the strength she had into the punch that never found its mark. The taller woman unleashed a devastating flipping crescent-kick and embedded her foot into the hairy fighter's jaw. The crowd went silent as the bloodied woman hit the floor. Then, as if the entire horde caught their breath, they erupted in cheers of excitement.

"The strength of a woman is not always appreciated. We are seen as weak and fragile."

Alli forced herself to pull her attention from the carnage in the cage to study the woman now standing beside her.

"We are stronger than they know."

She hesitated before asking, "They?"

"Men." The woman standing next to her was hidden beneath the dark cloak she kept pulled over her head. "This is the Den. It is where we come to prove our strength." Alli's eyes drifted back to the cage as the taller fighter raised her fist and enticed the crowd. "What about you? Are you strong?"

She blinked, and then blinked again before looking back to the woman. "Excuse me?" She felt a pang of insult at the insinuation of the question. She relaxed the tension within her fist and let out a slow breath. "I did not come here to fight. I am waiting for someone."

"Yes, I know. Me."

Alli's head snapped to the woman. She tried to get a better look at her face, but *that stupid cloak*. Then the woman lifted her gaze to meet hers and she knew those ruby eyes meant her no good.

The moment was interrupted by the announcer's voice. "Our next fighter is K'La. Do we have a challenger?!"

Before Alli could distance herself from the strange woman, she was grabbed by two males and dragged towards the cage.

EIGHT

Your Name Is Derrius

Narrock tried lifting his sagging head and was confused when he could not. He tugged at his arms and hissed as the joints of his shoulders threatened to snap. His eyes fluttered uncontrollably until the darkness returned and there was nothing. Each time his senses returned, he tried to sort out his current situation. The cold bite of steel around his wrists and ankles indicated he had been chained. The spoiled air and sticky wetness of the atmosphere a sign he was underground. With each pass through consciousness, the haze dissipated faster and his understanding grew.

"This bastard thinks he'll make a fool out of me does he?!

Well, I'll show him."

Narrock knew that grizzled voice, but from where?

"Gods' damned beast! Who the hell does he think he is?"

This time, as he awoke, he could smell the charring of wood. His body involuntarily twitched as embers of ash fell like snow onto his chest.

"Wake up, Derrius! Oh, wait, that's not your name, is it?"

Narrock fought to remain unbothered by this remark. He heard the taunt and reached for that kernel of anger, but his voice came out as nothing more than a whisper.

"That is not my name."

"I see my rennie was well spent. Your delay is wonderful. Who would have thought a few drops in your food and drink would produce such amazing results? Well, now you will know your place. And as I said before, your name is whatever I decide."

The menace of his laugh danced in Narrock's ears as the heat from the white-hot brand rode his nervous system, clearing out the haze and fully anchoring his mind back into reality. His gaze went from the brand to the man, and before he could bait the guard, the sizzling and singe of scorched flesh filled the air. Narrock's roar shook the entire coliseum.

"And now, boy. Your damn name is Derrius!"

NINE

Open Invitation

Alli fought to get free, but she could not break the grip of the two male figures. As they threw her into the den, the female approached the cage.

"These doors will not open until one of you has been knocked unconscious or rendered unable to fight. Don't worry, they don't allow killing, but it isn't illegal either." Then she walked away.

Alli scrambled to her feet and pressed her back against the cage. As she turned to face K'La, her stomach flipped, and she begged her body not to betray her. The fighter was enormous. Alli found that she barely came to K'la's shoulder. She was built like a smaller version of the males in the army. Dense muscle rested underneath her forearms and torso. Her lower body was sleek and powerful. She had the feminine grace of a noble, and yet her blood-lust was palpable. Yet despite her warrior demeanor, there was something still feminine about her. Alli was such a ball of emotions that she had not realized the distance K'La crossed when she pounced towards her. Somehow, she managed to dodge sideways avoiding her opponent's initial blow. Alli's body trembled and her eyes frantically roamed the Den for somebody to save her. She was not ready for this, not against this nightmare.

The outcome of the match is never determined by the one who does nothing. Her Master's words from her earlier lessons cut through the dysfunction of her thoughts.

Taking a deep breath, she readied herself. *I will not let fear hinder me.* She took her fighter's stance. Shifting her weight, she propelled herself towards K'La

Alli awoke the next morning bandaged up in her bed in the Routen's house. She did not remember much from the previous day. However, K'La's fist intimately making out with her face was something she could not forget. She struggled to sit up, but the pain from her bruises made her want to just stay

lying down. She was in so much pain that she had not even noticed the note in her hand. She unfolded the unfamiliar parchment.

> *Do not worry about your duties for today. Arrangements have been made. Hopefully, you learned a thing or two, as sparring is much more practical if you are looking to improve your skills. Before you begin to worry, I have said nothing to no one about your late night training sessions with Veronica. Should you actually desire to become a skilled fighter, you know where to go. And yes, you can take your friend. By the way, sorry for the secrecy, but when the time is right, a formal introduction will be in order.*

Just as she finished reading the note, there was a soft knock at the door. One of the servant girls pushed her way through the door with a small tray.

"I was told to bring this to you. It is supposed to help you feel better. You're to drink all of it," her eyes dropping to the floor.

"Thank you, you can leave it—"

"I am to watch you drink all of it," her eyes never leaving the floor.

Alli reluctantly took the brew and sniffed it. It smelt like piss and vomit defecated in a glass. Looking at the servant with eyes that asked, *Do I really have to drink this?*

She was met with answering eyes that said, *All of it.*

Not seeing any way out of it, she pinched her nose, pressed the cup up to her lips, tipped her head back, and chugged. It burned and tasted far worse than it smelled. She fought to keep the fowl liquid down. When her stomach settled, she handed the cup back to the servant. Once thoroughly satisfied Alli would not hurl the concoction over the floor, the servant made her way to the door.

"Oh, hopefully, you had a chance to relieve yourself."

Perplexed, Alli opened her mouth to ask a question, but before she could form the words, her eyelids slammed shut.

TEN

Deadly Through Silence

Narrock sat in the corner silently as everyone carried on. With the announcement of the tournament, all fights had been suspended. It had been a month since the last exhibition, and the only information they received was that the Reinzour wanted them to be in top shape at the start of the tournament. The hordes around him trained to focus on sharpening their skills. Others enjoyed the downtime engaging in idle conversation and grand wishes for what they hoped for if they won the tournament. Narrock and his kindred practiced through meditation.

The four males mostly always trained together. The past ten years honed them into deadly fighters who rarely felt challenged and hardly ever put real effort into their matches. Their focus shifted from surviving the Coliseum to defeating the Reinzour and returning home. To succeed they knew two things had to happen. First, they needed to release all of their upper limits—physical, emotional, mental, spiritual, and those of the heart. Those who master these disciplines transcend the boundaries of raw power, strength, endurance, and speed. They are fortified against physical and mental attacks. Focus and predictability sharpen along with adaptability. Release of the spiritual limits freed special skills, giving mortals the abilities of the celestial. Yet, above all, to break through the limits of the heart allowed complete control of mind, body, and soul. And second, they needed to understand how their enemy could control the elements.

Meditation was the answer to the first objective. Through it, they remained connected to Jhatar and kept their secrets hidden. No matter what they had to endure in this world, they would not lose this connection to what made them who they are. Enslavement had been the forge by which these warriors had been refined and shaped. Through their trials and adversity, they came to understand the deeper meanings of the truths revealed to them by their masters. They focused on shattering the limits of their abilities and reaching the heights that one day would allow them to free themselves from captivity. This had been their conclusion from the moment they were thrown in this pit and was the catalyst for the birth of the Four Dragons.

Narrock was vaguely aware of Kazwe's glare. He knew the older male did not like them and he did not care, and none of the dragons stirred as he approached and sat down beside them.

"What is wrong with you lot, always sitting in the corner looking off into space?"

Narrock ignored him but felt A'nark snap, "Hey asshole, mind leaving us alone."

Kazwe chuckled. "Big words from a bastard who'd rather stare into space instead of fight."

"Big words from a pretentious prick that's about to get his ass whooped."

Silence fell as the two exchanged deadly stares. Kazwe smirked. "Well, I guess we will have to see if your words have any bite."

"Yeah, I guess we will."

Just then, Ba'al and his guards burst through the door, "Alright you filthy little piss-ants, get in line."

Narrock's eyes opened as he sensed Ba'al. Forcing indifference onto his face, he made no effort to stand. He was keenly aware of the head guard at all times but struggled to keep his face neutral. His gaze fixed on the guard as he harassed the other fighters. He struggled to breathe as the pounding beneath his rib cage pulsed within his blood-filled eyes. The rage coursing through his body was so strong he barely noticed Jerren gripping his shoulder. Releasing a slow breath that hissed as it snaked between his gritted teeth, he took his position alongside the others.

"In one week, the Routen will inspect all of you and will each choose one of you to act as their proxy during the tournament."

As he began explaining what to expect, he walked down the line and stopped in front of Narrock. His eyes fixed on the brand. At the touch of his finger against the raised flesh, Narrock grimaced.

"Boy, have you finally learned your damn name?"

As he turned to gesture to the other guards, Narrock placed his hand around Ba'al's face and drove it through the ground in one swift motion. He took satisfaction in watching the guard's eyes roll to the back of his head before snapping back into place. Narrock's eyes, slits of predatorial fury, pinned the guard to the ground as the corner of his lips began to drift upward. While this happened, the other fighters created a human shield around them, no doubt wanting retribution for themselves even though they were too cowardly to seize it on their own. Raising his free hand, Narrock's nails pierced his own flesh. Slowly, he clawed across his chest, through the brand. He ensured droplets of his blood fell on Ba'al's face. Leaning forward, he whispered loud enough for him to hear.

"My name is Narrock."

Releasing the guard, he stood and leered as the other guards broke through the fighters and unleashed their wrath upon him.

ELEVEN

A New Challenger

Alli's head rattled against the metal cage causing her vision to see four opponents. Somehow, she managed to narrowly avoid a spartan kick as she jumped on her opponent's back. Her arm was like a python against the fighter's neck as she pulled back with all her strength. Blood streaked down her arm when her opponent sank her nails deep into her arm. The pain traveled through her nervous system and when it registered in her brain her grip almost faltered. Alli knew it was only a matter of time before the darkness would envelop her opponent's vision and the match would be over. So she shutdown the part of her brain that processed pain. That is when she felt the fighter's desperation kick in. The female swung her weight to the side, temporarily throwing Alli off balance, and when she thrust herself backward, she felt the unforgiving cage. She hit the cage so hard her teeth chattered violently, but her grip did not weaken. Again, she thrust, and again, and again. The next thrust found her vision failing, and her grip broke. Reaching for the back of her head, she felt something sticky and warm, and swore when she touched the two-inch gash before falling to her knees.

The other fighter collapsed to the ground gasping for breath. Alli struggled to get back to her feet, she wanted to end this fight quickly, but suddenly forgot about everything when her face was rocked to the side as her opponent's foot connected across her face. She saw everything in every direction, unable to focus on anything. Not hesitating, the fighter's foot connected with her stomach and she could no longer hold back the bile rising in her throat. At the sight of bile her opponent fought the urge to vomit and Alli used the distraction to strike. She flung herself at the fighter now on all fours. Twisting her torso, she landed a well-placed kick of her own, snapping bone. With everything she had left, Alli struck the side of her face with so much force that her opponent's skull bounced off the floor and her body followed, twitching uncontrollably.

The crowd erupted. The air filled with stomping feet, voracious hand clapping, and chants of "Hailey! Hailey! Hailey!"

Yet, Alli tuned it all out and focused all of her senses on the fighter lying motionless. The tremors stopped. She strained her eyes and ears, looking to see her chest rise even the slightest, listening for the shallowest of breaths, the faintest of heartbeats. Time stood still as she prayed she had not killed this fighter. And when she heard it, tears ran down her face as she rejoiced at the beauty of the rushing sound of life escaping from the injured woman's mouth.

Alli had been back to the den every day for the past week. She had not figured out who the cloaked figure was, but she was thankful Ishtar freed her from her servant responsibilities. She wanted to bring Ionis, but every time she left to fight, she just never asked her to come. For her, it had not been about the crowd, but ever since hope returned to her, after hearing her male kindred were still alive, she wanted to make sure she was someone who could stand by their side. They had been literally fighting for their lives for the past ten years, and even though she knew a week would not allow her to catch up, her first fight showed her just how far behind she was. And even though she knew Ionis would feel the same way, she still could never bring herself to share this with her. She had to prove that she was good enough to stand with them. Never once during their training had she ever bested Ionis. Alli needed this. She needed to be able to stand with her friend, not in her shadow.

Master Centrine, Narrock, Ionis, and the rest of her kindred would still be on Jhatar. They would all still be alive if only she could have stood that day. The scar on her leg began to thrum.

As the healers removed the unconscious fighter, Alli rose to her feet, "Who's next?!"

This had been her routine every night. Refusing to leave the cage until darkness claimed her. This earned her respect from some fighters, but many of the fighters found it disrespectful. A fighter was only supposed to fight once. It has always been that way. In their eyes, she was spitting on tradition. Never the less, the crowd loved it. Turning to the officiator, she asked again.

"Who's next!?"

"Are you sure? You've already had four fights." There was no hesitation in her eyes as she stared down the officiator. "Very well." he turned to the stable of fighters, "Are there any challengers?"

K'La began to make her way towards the cage, but before she could, she was halted. Alli watched as someone whispered in her ear. K'La turned away and returned to her seat. She felt the promise of defeat as she stared her down. Since K'La wiped the floor with her, Alli set her sights on defeating her. While she had not been given a chance at a rematch, she was somewhat relieved not to fight her in her current condition.

"We have a challenger!" the official announced.

Entering the cage, the challenger stood slightly taller than Alli and had a similar build. One side of her head was shaved, and on the other side, midnight black hair draped across her tatted skin down to her shoulder. This fighter was beautiful. But there was something about her that made Alli see herself. This world did not have people with such deep shades of hue, yet under the accented colors of the tattoos, this woman's almond skin sang of familiarity. Readying herself, she stared into those emerald eyes as the challenger starred back into her sapphire infused silver eyes, both searching for answers.

"Fight!"

In her current condition, her body felt like led. Every move she made was a delayed response from her brain. She knew she should have been able to avoid her attacks, but every blow connected. She should have seen it coming, but all she saw was darkness.

TWELVE

Unbreakable

I t had been three days since Narrock became the focus of Ba'al's torture, and he endured every moment of it staring the man directly in his face. He was sure he was in the same room as the last time but did not seem to care.

"You think you are tough, don't you *Derrius*? You see it's this arrogant attitude of yours I hate the most. You think you can do as you please, but you can't. Why can't you understand that?"

"Would you rather I become your subservient beast?"

Again, he flashed a grin at the guard. Fury overtook Ba'al, and he struck him across the face. Narrock allowed the thick metallic liquid to pool in his mouth before spitting at the guard's feet.

"Is that all you've got?" Sheer amusement painted his face.

Remembering how he received the scar now etched into his chest, he refused to eat or drink anything over the past three days. Instead, he trained his mental and physical hardening. The only time he would drop his ability was to take every blow Ba'al threw without flinching. Watching the guard's anger at not being able to break him brought him great joy.

"What happens when they come looking for this one?" another guard asked.

"They won't!" Ba'al snapped back. "I've marked this one as dead. You see, no one is coming looking for you, you piece of *shit*."

"You're nothing more than an impotent bastard that takes pleasure in gloating over the strong when you are the weakest one in the room," Narrock said.

This sent the guard into a blind fury. He felt each punch land. First his kidney, next his stomach, then his ribs, and finally his face.

"Know your place you, damned beast!"

Bringing his eyes to meet the guard, he grinned. By this

point, the other guard restrained him.

"You insolent bastard!"

Forcing his way free, Ba'al stretched out his hand and wrapped his magic around Narrock's head. As he closed his fist, Narrock thrashed as he felt wind coiling around his face before cutting off his circulation. Ba'al's wind slithered down his throat like a worm burrowing into a narrow hole before turning into a vacuum, sucking every ounce of air out of him. He finally released his magic when Narrock started to asphyxiate. This had been the first time he resorted to using his magic on him. As Narrock gasped desperately for air, he became aware of the real strength of this guard.

"You think you are special, don't you, Derrius?" Now it was the guard's turn to laugh. "You have no idea who you're messing with. If I wanted you dead, you'd be dead."

His words, mixed with the demonstration of his magic, which up until now meant nothing to him, made him realize the truth behind the threat. Still, he had not lost a single ember of defiance raging within his eyes.

"You can't break me. I am Narrock of Jhatar, a warrior of the Jazwon."

"We will see about that, *Derrius*."

And with that, the violent nature of his magic ruptured

in every direction.

The second guard watched from where he stood. It was not the depth of Ba'al's magic that caught his attention, but it was the fire that burned in Narrock's eyes. It was as if the guard's wind enraged the wildfire resting behind his amber eyes. He watched as the bound slave was pummeled with the fury of slashes and did not flinch. He marveled at the slave willing his body not to tremble. All the while Narrock maintained his fixated gaze on his torturer. On the outside, it looked as if the guard was in control, but the more his eyes recorded, the more he began to realize it was the slave who was in control.

"You will learn your place, and I will be the one to teach it to you."

Ba'al walked directly up to Narrock and concentrated the depth of his wind magic into a cyclone around his fist. As he took his stance, he hit the chained fighter with such force to his abdomen the wall behind him shattered, splintering shards of brick everywhere. Even with his hardening activated, the blow was enough to make him spew blood, yet he refused to give this bastard the satisfaction of hearing him scream ever again.

"Now, say it, boy. Tell me your damn name!"

With no hesitation. "Narrock."

This time, the guard redirected his power into his foot as he punted Narrock into the ceiling. Narrock could feel the breaking of bones as he came crashing back down to the ground.

"What is your name?!"

Raising his eyes to meet the guard's, he smiled, "My name is Narrock."

Ba'al stretched out both hands and clutched his wind around his neck. As he squeezed every ounce of life from his body, Narrock refused to yield to fear. He was not afraid of death nor was he afraid of this prick. So, he steadied his unbreakable will and peered into the depths of Ba'al's soul and bore his fangs.

Releasing his grip, Ba'al took a step back. He could not place it, but he felt like he realized what the other guard had came to understand earlier. Despite the broken bones and loss of blood, Narrock rose to his feet. Fear gripped the guard as his vision began playing tricks on him. Shaking his head to clear his vision, but the silhouette of a stalking predator would not fade.

"Who are you?" he asked. Not demanding an answer, but in sheer terror at the entity before him.

"I am Narrock," and as he made his final stand, his body plummeted to the ground.

Ba'al desperately struggled to tear his gaze away from the unconscious warrior. When he did, he turned to where the other guard stood and what color he still had vanished from his face. Standing behind the man was Reynuck of the Reinzour's personal guard.

"What the hell is going on?"

Reynuck had been standing in the entrance from the beginning. His fury kindled as this guard deliberately defied the Reinzour's orders. He watched as the guard lost control and unleashed his magic on the chained fighter. He watched as the slave was smashed through the wall, vaulted towards the ceiling, and he watched as Narrock stood and the guard stammered backward. Placing himself behind the other guard, Reynuck unraveled his magic and allowed his presence to be revealed. As he did this, he watched the guard's terror morph to pure dread.

"I believe I asked you a question," he said with deadly calm. The guard in front of him stood still as a statue, afraid that if he moved the Reinzour's personal guard would slay him where he stood.

"The slave defied our authority. We had to ensure the name of the Reinzour was protected."

The guard knew this answer was not wholly accurate, but he hoped it would provide an acceptable justification for their actions.

"Were your orders not clear? As the head guardsmen, you were to ensure no harm befall these fighters."

As Ba'al began to open his mouth, the silence in the room was broken as the other guard's head made contact with the floor.

Narrock had been faintly aware of the other presence standing just outside the door from the beginning. Although he thought nothing of it at first, he now came to realize how severe the situation truly was. He watched as the new male placed his hand around the hilt of his sword. He heard the sword whine as it awakened. He perceived the tension of the male's muscles as they propelled the sword so fast through the guard's neck that before any blood could cling to the blade Narrock heard the click of the sword being placed back into slumber. Neither guards had time to react, and to Narrock it seemed neither would have been able to. Using the shift of focus, Narrock desperately tried to gather what remaining strength he had. If this was to be his final stand, he would be sure to leave this world as a warrior.

Reynuck allowed his eyes to drift downward to where the guard's head rested. "I would think carefully before you try to deceive me." Harnessing the full fury of the ocean's wrath within his dark indigo eyes, he turned his gaze upon Ba'al.

"The bastard disrespected me! What the hell was I supposed to do? If I didn't do anything about it what would the other slaves think? This beast deserved to be taught a lesson." Reynuck stood still and allowed the guard to fester in fear.

"Very well, there is indeed logic to your action."

"Thank you sir, you are truly a man of good judgment—"

"However, I believe you said, what was it? Oh yes, that you marked him as dead and then called him a piece of shit. Did I get that right?"

Raising his hand, bright tendrils of flame reached hungrily from the tips of his fingers. It was strange watching them wade through the air until, in a mad dash, they raced to Ba'al. In an instant he incinerated into ash. In that moment, Narrock found himself back on Jhatar watching his Master's face melt away from her skull.

THIRTEEN

The Voids

V a'Luana returned to the Voids when the darkness claimed the sky. Her mission was simple, gather any intelligence useful to the Chief Elder. This had been her duty since she was born. She had been trained to be cunning, ruthless, and stealthy. Since the colonizers invaded their planet over two hundred years ago, the Voidwalkers as they were called, have been trying to take it back. For the past five years, Va'Luana had been meeting with sources within the city. Most of the news she would receive was inconsequential, but every now and then she would obtain valuable information.

The tip she received this time was regarding a fighter at

the Den. Her informant relayed information about the girl's first encounter and how she was thrown into the cage. While the tip on the girl meant nothing to her, it was the other players that did. They described a cloaked woman and two males who accompanied the girl. When she pressed for more information, the details of the fight were described, as was the fact the girl was returned to the inner sanctum of the city by the cloaked woman. The last bit of information was that the girl had become a regular. She returned each day to fight until she had either been knocked out or unable to fight.

"What does this girl look like?" she asked.

The informant hesitated. "Just like you."

These words left her confused. There could not be another girl like her on this planet. It was impossible. Her breath hitched and her mind raced in a thousand different directions when she saw this girl who shared her features. She was not ready to believe it, even though her eyes confirmed what her mind would not register. So she watched the honey-skinned girl fight, and when she reached the point she could no longer battle, Va'Luana approached the cage. She had no intentions of fighting, but she knew she could at least get close enough to see the girl without drawing attention to herself. She expected the match to be denied after watching the other fighter be turned away, but to her surprise, they cued the fight.

75

"Where is the Chief Elder?" she demanded.

The scout studied her for a moment before pointing in the distance. Nodding her head, she turned and walked away. There was something majestic about the crest of this hill. It was said that this was the place where every ruler was anointed and there, standing at the precipice, was the Elder, paying his respects to the goddess of the night.

"Val, you rarely come and see me anymore," the old man smiled and gestured for her to join him.

"I'm sorry. With everything trusted to me, I...I just don't want to let anyone down."

There was truth to that, but she also wanted to show him she was not a burden. She had no idea where she came from. All she knew was that her mother beseeched the Voidwalkers to take her in before disappearing. The Chief has been like a father to her, and lately, she felt she was not contributing anything to the fight. As the camp's spymaster, it was her job to collect intelligence, but what she found over the past month or so was not worth a pot to piss in.

As he studied her, he leaned forward and placed his palm on her forehead. "The young are responsible only to live my child." Wanting to change the conversation quickly, Va'Luana opened her mouth to speak, but before she could say anything, the Chief continued. "Care for some tea? I believe this may be my finest brew yet?"

"Chief, I—"

"I've been alive for a very long time. I have spent many years perfecting this gift. To think purpose is affected by ingredients that make the same substance." He arranged two cups beside the pot and waited. "We were all created to be equal; yet, conquest and revenge, elitism and greed, heritage and the lack thereof have forced us into a world where the foundation of peace is challenged."

This was the other reason she often avoided the Chief. His old-man stories laced with lessons tended to last longer than she felt like listening. He clapped his hands to draw her attention.

"Val, what do you think separates us from those who stole our home?"

"Does it matter?"

"Of course it does," he said with a hint of disappointment.

"I don't know, and I don't care. All I know is *they*," gesturing vaguely somewhere outside the Void, "have taken our home, and I want it back."

"Val, you cannot become so blinded by what you seek that you do not take the time to consider this question."

"This is a waste of time. I will just report my findings to the Captain." Moving to get up, Va'Luana felt his firm grip around her arm.

While he was an old man, the intensity of his inner power was far superior to anyone else within the Voidwalkers or any of the Watchers she met in the city.

Releasing a deep sigh, she conceded. "I'm sorry. I just don't understand."

Relaxing his grip, he patiently explained. "Ignorance and fear. These are two of the most dangerous enemies we face. When they become our masters, we lose the ability to be rational, and everything we do is guided by selfish ambition or gain. One day you will understand these words, but until then, what is it you wish to share?"

Waiting for her to speak, he poured the two cups and passed one to her. This was his calming tea. She could tell by the scent of lavender and honey. She blew it before taking a sip. As it hit her tongue, she could taste the sweet floral melody along with the hint of apple. The tension on her mind melted away as the tea passed through her system, and her muscles eased slightly. Opening her eyes, Val turned to the Chief.

"Today I saw a girl who looked like me." She watched as his brow raised before it fell.

"What do you mean, like you?" he took a sip of his tea.

"Exactly what I said, she looks just like me."

"Where did you see her?" Setting his tea down, he turned his full attention to her.

Hesitating. "It was at the Den."

She knew this answer would bring ire from the Chief as he has made it clear he did not want her going to that place. But when he said nothing, she continued.

"There's more, I fought her."

"You did what!" his voice echoed as he was now standing.

Tea spilled over the lip of the cup as her hands quivered in response to his anger. "I, I only went to watch after one of my sources told me about it. I wanted to see with my own eyes. They told me when she comes that she fights until she can't fight anymore. So, I waited until she could not fight before I stepped in to face her. It was over quickly." She was hoping that if she filled him in with some of the details that he would not be as mad.

"Stupid girl!" Several moments passed before he spoke again. "Your duty is to infiltrate the city and collect information that is helpful to us and to do it covertly."

"Chief, I know! But, this could be the chance we have

79

been waiting for."

Raising his hand, the Chief ordered her silence. He walked to a massive tree to rest his head. When he stilled his soul, he turned towards Val. She braced herself for what was to come as the warmth of his breath against the frigid night made it seem as if he was breathing smoke.

"Explain yourself."

Va'Luana explained everything to the Chief. She told him about the woman who brought her, the guards that followed, how the girl became stronger as a fighter over the few days at the Den, and why she believed they should try to recruit her.

"The woman and guards, whose Shadow are they?" the Chief inquired.

"The woman, I don't know. She had been cautious not to show her face, but the guards returned her to the house of Routen Ishtar."

Returning to sit by her side. "How do we know she can be trusted?"

Va'Luana paused for a moment, thinking back to her brief encounter with the girl. She set her emerald eyes on his precious hazel eyes.

"Because when I looked at her, I saw me."

She was unsure if the Chief would understand what she was saying, but it was all she could think of. Even though she could not explain it, Va'Luana knew she saw this girl possessed the same desire for freedom that she had.

After he considered everything she told him, the Chief massaged his temples. "Go get the captain, and we will see what she thinks of this."

Excitement overtook her, and as she shot to her feet to race off to get the Captain, the Chief called after her.

"Val."

She stopped and turned to the Chief.

"You did well."

She smiled and turned for the captain's quarters.

FOURTEEN

Serpents of the Past

Alli woke with a jolt. Her last memory was like looking in a mirror. As she sat up in the bed, the dreadful chorus of her muscles sang with great displeasure. She hurt everywhere. A break, and much needed rest were definitely in her future.

Just as she was considering, the small pitter-patter of rain began to play against her window. Closing her eyes, Alli allowed the beautiful crescendo to relax her mind. She always found herself at the most peace during the rain. Yet, while the rain granted her momentary tranquility, it also, over the last few years, opened the wounds buried deep within her heart.

It had been a night just like this when Alli was around

three. She pressed against the door slowly, not wanting to alert her mother as they were not allowed to go out in the rain. She understood it was dangerous, according to her mother, but to her, the crisp cool crystals were a relief from the pain of her father leaving. However, tonight was different. Tilting her face towards the sky, the celestials seemed to share in her sorrow as her tears and theirs fell at the same pace, the pain in her heart refusing to subside. She recalled hearing someone calling after her but struggled to make out who. The monstrous shouts from the stratosphere were deafening, and the cold droplets of ice fell so rapidly that the ground was covered with a mist of frost. Fear gripped her. Heart racing, her ragged breathing made it almost impossible to dislodge the malignant lump in her throat. Yet, despite the growing desire to allow the storm to carry her away, she continued to hear someone screaming her name. Just as her memory was connecting the voice with an image, a flashing serpent snaked down from the sky, lighting everything in its path as it reared its fangs and struck her with all its might.

A tear ran down her cheek. She could never remember anything before this. Wiped were her memories of the love of a family, the face of her mother, the embrace of her father all gone. Another chased after the first. Then her thoughts turned to Master Centrine. The serpent's bite left her sprawled in a puddle threatening to drown her. She could not tell if the pool was created from the rain or if it had been the collection of her tears. And just as she was ready to breathe her last breath, she felt firm but gentle hands lift her from where she lay. Her body no longer felt cold because whatever cradled her burned bright as a furnace. Batting her eyes to clear the frosted tears, she saw Master Centrine.

Another tear chased the first as she reminisced about her earliest memory. She did not know this woman, but she seemed so familiar. Just then, that same flashing serpent flashed its fangs again. This time, when it struck, Alli was back on Jhatar. She stood there as her master lay in a lake of blood. The dams in her eyes broke, and she wept uncontrollably. The rate of tears exceeded the tempo of the water droplets against the window. As she stood there, her master's gaze forever locked on her, sorrow embraced her, and rocked her gently into a deep sleep.

She next woke, not to the tapping of the rain, but to the unfamiliar steps of someone in her room. Still dazed from slumber, Alli grasped for consciousness as she felt small hands grasp around her wrist and the touch of cold metal graze across her skin. Heart racing, Alli pushed her assailant off her, and she landed on the ground with a thud. In an instant, Alli was on her feet, but not in time to stop the individual, who attempted to bind her, from fleeing out the door past the other person who blocked the path. She stared at him. It was obvious to her this man was a guard by his wide frame and rigid posture, but she could not understand why he let someone into her room.

"Who are you? And why are you here?"

"Come now, I'm a little disappointed you don't remember me, Hailey. Or is it Allister? I'm so confused."

It was still a few hours before sunrise. Alli angled her head in an attempt to make out his face. She cursed when she realized he understood what she was doing and he shifted his body back into the darkness.

"Oh, no you don't. Not that easy."

"What do you want from me?"

"From you? I think it's more about what *you* want from *me*."

The man took a step forward. His movement was slow, calculated. Alli was so focused on him that she did not realize her feet became tangled in her bedding. As she stepped backward, her foot slipped. Stretching her hands to the floor to brace herself, she winched in pain when she landed awkwardly on the ground. Suddenly, she felt his weight pinning her down, and she froze as his sadistic laugh echoed in her ears.

"Ever since I saw the way you looked at *him*, I've wanted you." He held her arms firmly against the floor.

She squirmed, trying to free herself. All the while, her mind raced to piece together who he was. Then she felt it. The hard muscle against her navel began to grow, and her heart stopped.

"Help—" she cried, but before she could get the words out, she felt his calloused fingers around her throat as if she was the hilt of a sword.

"Feisty are we? Well, I'm not looking for a show tonight, but I promise to be gentle." Hovering his mouth to her ear, he whispered, "Don't worry, I won't make you bleed like your friend unless you want to."

Her thoughts raced, desperate to remember. And before fear could paralyze her, she heard her master.

"Death awaits those who cannot overcome their inability to act."

She willed her mind to be quiet, her pulse to drawl, and she welcomed the calming storm to seize her.

"I see you're done fighting." He said, as she sprung forward wrapping her arms around him. "Oh, so you do want this?"

Feeling him relax, she cinched her grip and launched herself backward. As she did, Alli heard the loud thud of his head bouncing off the ground. Her right leg trapped his left leg while simultaneously freeing her right arm and pinning his left arm against her side. Then, driving her left foot into the ground, she exploded every ounce of strength she could harness straight up, throwing her last remaining force through her left arm as she flipped onto his chest. With his mount reversed, she raised her fist and brought down Hell's wrath. Again and again, she pounded his face as bone broke and the ruggedness of his face was reduced to a pile of mangled flesh. She tapped into that well of primal desire to protect herself, mixed with a need for retribution, that she had not even felt the guards as they pulled her from her attacker's limp body. And while tears still ran down her face, the corners of her lips twitched upward as she left him in a pool of his own blood.

FIFTEEN

Lies and Betrayal

Alli had no idea how long she had been locked away since obliterating the guard's face, but she did know this space was cramped. She had been down here for several hours and barely had any room to even lie down. Left to her own devices, she began to question her decision to dismantle the guard's face. One side made its case against the stupid act of violence while the warrior demanded she not regret her decision. As much as she agreed with the latter, the despair of the unknown made her feel as if she was going to vomit. This internal conflict continued until she was startled by the scrapping of a key in the lock to her cell. The door screeched as it was pulled open. Momentarily blinded by the rushing river of light breaking through the door, she shielded her eyes and squinted trying to readjust her vision. Just as everything was coming into focus, terror overtook her. Standing on the other side of the door was Dendaron, the guard from last night.

"Gods be damned, this is the girly that did that to you?" one of the guards asked mockingly. "Shit, maybe you should have left this one alone."

"Keep talking and I swear I will beat the hell out of you—"

"Out of me? I'm surprised you can still shit out your mouth after what she did to you." Rolling his head back, the guard released a laugh so insulting that Dendaron charged him.

"Enough!" another man commanded. With just one word, both soldiers discontinued.

So he must be in charge, she thought.

"Hailey, I apologize for my subordinates' behavior. Would you please come with us?" his words more of a statement than a question.

As she crawled out of the tiny space, Dendaron spat on the ground right in front of her.

"Bitch," he whispered.

Alli fought to maintain control of her body. She willed

her muscles to relax and demanded herself not to show the slightest bit of fear. Silencing the trembling of her being, she rose from the ground without a word.

Every step she took exuded power in the presence of her attacker. Even though under the surface, she knew it was just an act. Walking down the familiar hallway, Alli could not help but explore the feelings she first felt and wished the circumstances for her second visit had been different. Although the head on the trident still freaked her out, she managed not to show it. When they reached the Routen's study, they were greeted by Brista, who gracefully opened the door and returned to setup in the receiving area. The Routen ordered the kitchen to bring an extravagant array of hors d'oeuvres. Eyeing the piles of food, she suddenly remembered she had not eaten in a while. Then her gaze fell on Brista. She thought it unusual, that the usually arrogant Brista seemed much more reserved today.

Figures, we are in the Routen's study, she said to herself.

Brushing it aside, she looked around the study seeing more details than she had the last time. Then she remembered what happened to Ionis when they were here. She shuttered.

When Brista finished setting up, she knelt down and reached under the table to withdraw a drying cloth. Walking behind the Routen's desk, she poured a drink and moved to place herself beside a door Alli had not recognized until now. Brista knocked once and positioned herself five steps in front of the door. After a moment, Ishtar emerged wearing low hugging pants and sweat. When he took the drink, Alli watched as he brought the glass to his lips and breathed in the liquid. She could not shake the sudden wish for him to drink all of her. *Strange.* She should not feel like this. Not after what happened last night. In fact, she should be repulsed, but Alli could not pull her gaze away. An unexpected bead of sweat racing down the side of his face caught her attention. As it gathered itself over the strong edge of his clean-shaved jawline, it jumped. Her honed eyes followed the bead down his broad chest and chiseled abdomen, and as it passed the V of his waistline, all the color drained from her face. Finishing the drink, Ishtar took the drying cloth and wiped the sweat from his body, all the while holding her gaze with his silver frost-dusted eyes.

"Thank you Brista, you may take your position over there," gesturing with a slight nod of his head.

Brista entered a low curtsy before taking her post. As he walked across the study, Alli felt her heart change tempo. Each step closer he took, she found her breathing deepen. Her body began to shake as she was overwhelmed by her desire to warm his snow-like flesh, the grip of fear of what he has yet to do to her, and the traumatic events of last night. When he reached his desk, he opened the armoire to retrieve a shirt before sitting down. Turning to face her, Ishtar slid the cloth over his naked chest and leaned back in his chair. She did not know what to make of the sadness that filled her now that he was covered.

"Dendaron, please explain to me what happened last night," his gaze still fixed on her.

"This bitch—" as soon as the word came out of his mouth, he instantly regretted it.

"You dare speak that way in my presence?" Ishtar's nails dug into the wood.

"My lord, please forgive me. I meant no disrespect." He entered into a deep bow. When nothing else was said, he slowly stood and continued. He explained how he was summoned to her room, and when he refused, she decided to attack him.

"That is not true!" The Routen's eyes, which remained fixed on her, shifted to Dendaron and then back to her.

"You claim my Toultyn is lying?"

"Yes," she said, only hesitating for a second.

"There is a steep penalty for challenging the authority of my men." Turning his attention to the dismantled face of Dendaron. "Is there anything else you would like to add?" Shaking his head, Dendaron ended his statement. "It is forbidden for any of the servants of this house not born of Valencian blood to touch any member of my house unless I wish it."

"I did not ask that lying coward to my room. He attacked me!" she said fighting the tears forming in her eyes.

Anger washed over Ishtar's face, and suddenly she knew her fate. "Sit down," he whispered. Without any resistance, she sat in the chair facing the Routen. "Then tell me what happened?"

Figuring he already knew about the Den, she recounted the entire story. Everything from going unconscious at the Den and the memory of her late master to waking up to someone trying to bind her, and ending with the pleasure she took in leaving the guard in a pool of his own blood.

"I never asked him to my room."

Sitting back in his chair, Ishtar analyzed Alli's testimony. Looking from Dendaron to Alli, and back to Dendaron, Ishtar spoke. "Is it true? Did you first see her in my study?" Dendaron nodded. "I see. Where did you next see her?"

Caught off guard by the question, he stammered for a response. "I don't remember."

"Hailey, tell me. Out of curiosity, how many of my men have you opened your legs to?"

She jumped to her feet. "My lord, I have done no such
93

thing." Her honey skin flushed red before she quickly took her seat, eyes glued to the floor.

"Have you ever spread your legs for a male?"

At this, she was no longer able to hold back the tears that flooded her eyes. "My lord, I have done no such thing."

Turning to the drawer behind him, Ishtar reached inside and pulled out a dagger. Placing it on the desk, he looked at her as fear choked every emotion she had in her throat.

"Dendaron, are you aware that everything in this house is my property?" The guard nodded. "And yet, you would dare touch what belongs to me without my permission."

"My lord, you trust this bitch over me!" Ishtar's eyes slowly traveled to Dendaron.

"I believe that is the second instance you have said that."

Two Toultyn appeared behind Dendaron grasping both his arms and kicking out his knees. Pinning him to the floor, a third Toultyn grabbed a fist-full of his hair and yanked his neck back, forcing his mouth open. Alli watched Ishtar stand and walk to where Dendaron was held. Reaching inside his mouth, Ishtar pulled his tongue as far as he could and with one swift cut, he dropped Dendaron's tongue to the floor. She closed her eyes and looked away, her stomach in her throat.

"I've told you, everything in this house is my possession.

Do you really believe you could fool me?" Ishtar returned to lean against his desk. "You mentioned a second person. Would you like to know who it was?" using the tip of the knife to picked at the underside of his fingernail.

This took Alli by surprise. She was still trying to come to terms with the blood-stained dagger in his hand. He pushed off the desk and bent down. His face was so close she only needed to tilt her head slightly, and the warmth of his lips would have touched against hers. He dropped the knife in her lap and set his eyes to the distance. Alli followed his gaze. Anger boiled as she realized he was looking at Brista.

"You were the one who tried to tie me up?" Tears began to well in Brista's eyes.

"Well, Hailey, who would you like to kill first? Your attacker? Or the conspirator?"

The shock of this revelation overtook her1 as she sat there motionless. "How could you?"

Several moments passed as she said nothing eying the blade resting on her thighs. She sat there, her senses dulled until she felt Ishtar run his hand across her knee, grazing gently over her inner thigh. He grabbed the knife. With that, her body took on a different kind of shock as her sapphire eyes lost themselves within his. Flicking his wrist, the dagger he held now embedded itself deep in Brista's esophagus. Alli could not hear Brista's muffled scream as blood bubbled from her mouth. Instead, she watched as his eyes cut to Dendaron. Ishtar's anger swelled as his magical pressure began to fill the room. She never felt anything like this in her life. This immense pressure was suffocating. With every step he took towards Dendaron, it multiplied. She watched as everyone became so paralyzed by fear and wondered what Dendaron felt as the Routen's hand wrap around his skull. She could not look away as his grip shredded through flesh, bone, and brain matter.

SIXTEEN

A Warning

Narrock was conflicted as he sat in the infirmary alone. There were so many people that needed treatment and many already died when something could have been done. Even though he knew why, it still pained him to receive this level of care while others suffered.

It had been days since he last saw the man who robbed him of the satisfaction of killing Ba'al. He could not help but wonder all this time, *who was he?* Narrock gritted his teeth and slightly curled his lips over his teeth remembering. He assumed Ba'al's torture made it difficult for him to clearly see the man, but he could not shake the feeling it was something else that blinded him. He flexed his muscles from his shoulders to his fingers as his arms rested on his knees. He remembered the overwhelming pressure he felt just before the guard was turned to ash. All this time, he had seen glimpses of this extraordinary power they wielded—as if they were celestials—but he has never been able to understand how these men obtained the abilities of what they called gods. No one on their world possessed the knowledge to control the elements, *so how is it that they do?*

On Jhatar, he understood the gifting received for mastering the spiritual uppers, but this...this was something much different. Being victimized by Ba'al, feeling suffocated by that man. He knew that if he was to continue protecting his kindred and possibly find a way off this miserable planet, he would have to figure out how to steal this power and harness it for himself.

"I'm glad to see you are doing better," a voice said, cutting through his thoughts.

Narrock turned his attention to the healer. She had been by his side seeing to his every need. Being the first time he has been allowed this close to a female since being thrown in the Coliseum, her very presence called to the animalistic instincts that lay dormant deep within. She was nothing special to look at. The paleness of her skin told him she was native to this place, but every time she touched him, he found himself bewitched by the softness of her skin. He could often feel the increase of her pulse as she checked his progress, and he had no shame allowing her to see exactly what she was doing to him. Especially since, he could detect she oozed a strong desire for what he might feel like. Sometimes it disgusted him, the thoughts running through his mind. Of what he would do to her if no one were around and if she was Jazwon instead of Valencian. But he also understood this was built into his system, even though he would never act upon it.

"You will be returning to the others this evening," she said with a hint of disappointment.

"May I ask you a question?" Returning her eyes to his, she leaned in with anticipation. "The man with the ability to control fire, who is he?"

"Well, before I answer, you should put that away, you're not quite my type." Narrock's eyes shot to the door as the healer jumped from where she sat. "Not that I care, but you do know this one is not for mating...don't you?" Reynuck's brow rose slightly.

"My lord, I only saw to his injuries. He is ready for discharge at your leisure," she said still trying to gather her composure.

"Thank you, you may go."

They both watched as the healer gathered herself and left.

"Now then," returning his focus to Narrock, "why is it that you inquire about me?"

Narrock held the male's gaze. "Why did you spare me and kill your own?"

"First of all, do not flatter yourself. I did not save you," he said sardonically. "Second, anyone who disregards the Reinzour's sovereignty is not 'one of my own,' as you say."

There was definitely something different about this male. Narrock thought it was his injuries that impeded his view of the man, but now he suspected otherwise.

"Who are you, and why can't I see you?"

For a moment, Reynuck's face flickered with something like surprise before falling back beneath the mask of disinterest. "My name is of no concern to you. Now tell me something, why was that guard torturing you?"

"Maybe you should have asked him before you killed him."

Chuckling, "I'm glad to see you find this amusing, but I am not as nice as Ba'al so don't waste my time. Now answer my question."

Considering the consequences of his response, Narrock decided to tell the man all that happened. When he seemed satisfied, the man instructed him to gather his things. He was being returned to the Coliseum.

"Tomorrow, you will be presented before the Routen." Narrock scoffed at the thought of being paraded around like some show thing. "They are the most powerful commanders on this planet. If you value your life, do not piss them off. I may not be able to touch you, but they will kill you."

SEVENTEEN

A Forgotten Warrior

The day of the fighter auction was finally here. The Coliseum was a beehive of action. Before the day even begun, all the fighters were ordered to be bathed and have all body hair shaved except their heads. After they had been washed and shaved, they were lathered with the finest oils and conditioners. The scent of cedar, nutmeg, cypress, and mint filled the air. Narrock's nose was in overdrive as they rubbed him down with sage oils to complement his burnt woodsy scent. Then they were inspected to ensure all their bruises and wounds healed properly. Once cleared, they were issued a white satin blouse and matching trousers, nothing else. The choir of clanking chains filled the air as they were herded from the holding area onto transport vehicles to be transferred to the staging areas prepared to receive the Reinzour and the Routen. One by one, they were to be auctioned to the Routen as representative fighters, with the winner bringing good favor and blessing to their house. It was also the first time he realized there were faces he never saw before. After a moment of thought it did not seem strange anymore. Of course there would be other fighting prisons.

Any ideas of escape or resistance had been quickly discouraged when one fighter's attempt was brutally ended. Narrock watched them beat him and drag him away. As they rounded the corner, he fought back the pain in his heart as his eyes traveled along the streaks of blood back to where the fighter first stood.

Am I really that much of a coward that I did nothing? Narrock wondered. In the end, his thoughts yielded to the ever-present truth. *There is nothing I could've done for that fighter, or anyone. Not until I find a way to acquire the power these people wield.*

While they were in the Coliseum, the guards were forbidden to use magic to harm them. This caused some of the fighters to believe they were weak. Today, however, this restriction had been lifted, and the guards were responsible for the peace of the event and the protection of the Reinzour. Twenty-four Routen were to place bids today. Narrock did not have to count to know there were more fighters here than the Routen could bid for. Warily dismissing the matter, he went back to trying to understand why all of this was necessary. The announcer's opening remarks cut through his thoughts.

"What a load of crap this is. Are they really going to parade us in front of these so-called commanders as if we are livestock?" A'nark asked.

"Listen, we have always focused on survival. No matter how we feel or what goes on, we must survive. Got it?"

The four dragons all took turns looking into one another's eyes and nodded in agreement.

"You are my brothers. We have survived this far, and it doesn't change today," Bhurron said, understanding the weight of what was about to happen.

As they turned their attention back to the announcer, they listened to the explanation of the rules. After explaining the provisions of the tournament came the process of the auction.

"Now, may I present to you his holiness, our Reinzour."

All the sound had been sucked out of the room as everyone stood to their feet placing their fists against their hearts while executing a slight bow. The Reinzour strolled down the aisle to the front of the room. While none of the fighters could see him, they all felt the sheer weight of his magic pressure emanating throughout the entire area.

"Bring out the fighters!" he commanded.

All the fighters were ushered out to stand before the Reinzour. Narrock knew the Routen were all curtailing their power because he remembered how powerful the male with the fire's felt. Comparing the Reinzour's to theirs, he understood just how dangerous the man standing in front of everyone was. He was sure this was not the truth of his pressure. For a moment, their eyes met. It felt like an eternity. The man was built like a warship. His face, chiseled from bloodshed and conquest, looked down on everyone as if he had no rival. His rusted hair rested just over his broad frame and with those hazel eyes promising death, Narrock looked away first.

"Today, one of you attempted to embarrass me." The Reinzour's Shadows dragged a bloodied fighter to the middle of the stage. Narrock recognized him from his earlier attempt at rebellion. "I do not take kindly to my good will being spat on."

With each word, the Reinzour's pressure continued to grow. Several fighters found themselves unable to keep their balance and their knees went crashing to the ground. Others were visibly struggling to remain standing. Narrock and the three expanded their senses to perceive the reactions of the Routen. Not a single one of them so much as trembled under this pressure. As if all of them had the same idea of not drawing attention to themselves, the four dragons mimicked the reaction of the other fighters.

Ishtar had been watching the four males since they were brought before the Reinzour. He noticed how they seemed unfazed and how they seemed to be putting on a show to fit in. This caused him to smirk. He was sure that no matter what, he had to have one of them as his representative.

"You will serve as an example today of what will happen if any of your fellow slaves get the same idea."

The maimed fighter, now floating in the air, began bellowing out in pain as each of his limbs were wrenched out of place. The room filled with the sound of splintering bones. Blood poured out of every opening in his body until it had all been rung out onto the stage. Finally, what was left of his lifeless body simply turned to dust and disintegrated into nothing.

"Let this be the last any of you decide to cross me."

And with that, the fighters were ushered back into the staging area while the Reinzour addressed the Routen. When he finished speaking, the Routen stood again for his departure. One by one, each fighter was brought out, stripped down to their bare skin, and forced to stand in the center of the bloodstained stage. The Routens took turns demanding the fighter perform specific actions. Once they had been satisfied, the bidding began.

Several of the Routen settled quickly upon their desired proxy the moment bidding opened. The abundance of fighters meant there were very few contested bids—that is, until it was Kazwe's turn. Ishtar sat back as the other Routen entered heated confrontation regarding who would own the rights of this fighter. From what he heard, this was the leader of the slaves and was ruthless when engaged in battle. This warrior had been battle-tested and would be an asset to anyone who would win his services. But Ishtar watched as even he buckled at the pressure of the Reinzour. Not caring about the outcome of this endeavor, he closed his eyes and waited from the males he deemed worthy. The first was A'nark, whose name was Edgar; then Bhurron whose name was Philip; followed by Jerren, whose name was Jase. There was not a lot of clamor surrounding these fighters. He readied his bid as Bhurron entered, but when the only female Routen placed her bid, he decided he would wait to see the last male. Finally, Derrius was brought to the stage. He wasted no time placing his bid on him. Many of the Routen began to laugh and question Ishtar's sanity. But he knew they only saw his diminished stature and scar-riddled body. Yet he did not care. He knew this was the fighter who was destined to move him to the Reinzour's second-in-command and make him the Chief of Commanders. When no one else bid, Ishtar gathered his things and exited the hall.

Narrock never felt so degraded in his life. Forced to stand there, naked, and in the blood of the fighter who had been put on display by this Reinzour. He clenched his fist until he drew blood as he fought to keep his anger at bay. Once he'd picked up his clothes and walked off the stage, he sent his fist hurling through the stone wall leading back to the staging area. When he returned, the entire room was filled with shame and defeat, all except for Kazwe. His elation only served to make everyone else feel more dejected.

"Why the hell are you all sandbagging? Don't you realize we are finally going to get out of this place?"

"At what price?" another male asked.

"I have never been so humiliated in my life," said another.

"Here's some advice. You ready? Get. The hell. Over it! You're all acting like a bunch of damned babies," Kazwe said looking down on all of them.

Narrock put on his clothes, and he reflected on what Kazwe said. He acknowledged the truth of his words, but the question the other fighter asked steadily rang in his soul. *What have we traded?* He thought to himself. He thought about the blood they had to stand in.

"The fighter no one will ever remember died taking a stand. He died a warrior's death while the rest of us cowered to our oppressor. We are not warriors. We're cowards."

Narrock had not realized he was speaking until the silence of the room forced him to look up. These words that were supposed to have been part of a private conversation within himself touched every male in the room.

"His name was Asher," Kazwe said, lowering his head.

Then unclenching his fist, he laid a strand of Asher's blood-soaked garment in the center of the room. Every warrior in that room stood in respect, and when Kazwe knelt, they all knelt and remained that way until they were summoned by their respective Routen.

The four dragons agreed there was nothing worth taking from this place to their next destination. Instead, they gathered together in the make-shift memorial for the fallen warrior. This would be the last time they would see each other for a while. There were no words exchanged. They each grasped the arm of the one beside them in a locking circle. As was their custom, they turned to the oldest.

"I leave you with one word. Survive," Bhurron said.

One by one, they took turns echoing the command of the elder. Survive. Then they headed their separate ways. Narrock entered the clearing where he was supposed to meet with Ishtar. As he approached, he noticed two other cloaked figures with him. Releasing his senses, he could perceive that one of the individuals was trembling with an elevated pulse, female. The other stood with the same cold, calculated stance as the Routen. Also female. Slowing his gate, Narrock's instincts began to tell him to beware. Just as he stopped, one of the cloaked females ripped away her hood and attacked.

EIGHTEEN

Unleashed

Alli had been excited to join Ishtar ever since they left his territory in Valencia-Cardinal. She found herself awestruck over the five-day trip to Valencia-Parish. Traveling through the provinces, she was reminded of the beautiful foliage that blanketed her homeland. Her eyes traced the massive trees from the forest floor to where their large canopies blotted out the heavens. The scent of pine flowed through her nostrils and was flushed by the crisp salty coolness of the lakes and rivers. She watched as the winged creatures soared, and her breath escaped as she watched a majestic four-legged beast give birth. While the mother was beautiful, the slimy pile of fur was not. Even after crossing the river into Valencia-Commonwealth, Alli continued to take in the beauty of Valencia. When they emerged onto the open plain, she was no longer a slave in a foreign place. Under the impressive depth of the night sky and the billions of shiny jewels dancing across the massive sea of black, for a moment, she was home on Jhatar.

When they reached Valencia-Parish, she was surprised to see Ishtar stopped to pick up a stranger. The coach rocked and swayed when she entered. Sitting next to the Routen, they began discussing their plans. Alli looked out the window. She tried to conceal her quick glances as she tried to figure out who this woman was. Eventually, she gave up and instead listened to them discuss all the fighters up for auction and the measures she taken to provide the best chance for Ishtar to win his prize. She could only hope they were discussing one of her kindred as the prize. Ishtar had not spoken to her about them since he brought her to his study all those weeks ago. And now, the hope she had been trying to push aside was clawing its way to the top, ready to burst out of her chest. The carriage jolted as it came to a stop, flinging her harmlessly against the plush cushion seat. Exiting the coach, Ishtar commanded the two women to remain as he made his way to the hall.

It was finished. Ishtar left the auction hall and claimed

his prize. Returning to his coach, he unleashed a devilish smile. Alli felt her heart skip a beat and quickly worked to hide the look of desire that flashed across her face.

"Well, was he everything you expected?" the woman asked with a self-satisfied smirk.

There was something familiar about her voice. The entire time, she tried to remember how she knew this woman, but the way she asked this question sent Alli's mind into a fury. She thought back to the schoolhouse, to the hall at the Routen's house. Nothing. Every place that came to mind did not fit and then she remembered.

"I cannot say I was disappointed with what I saw. However, the real test is yet to come." Turning to Alli. "Under no circumstance are you permitted from taking off your cloak. If you choose to disobey my order, I will end you." Alli understood at once and nodded. She said nothing as she followed Ishtar and the woman as they exited the coach.

Alli stood there as tears pooled at the bottom of her eyes. There, walking up the hill to where they were standing was Narrock. The water in those pools began to crest as she took in every detail. He was taller than she remembered, and there was not a single inch of his body that was not untouched by a sculptor's knife. Seeing his long braided locs instantly took her back to the training grounds where Master Centrine... she stopped the thought forming and focused on the present. Those pools now turned to rivers. Not just at his familiar sienna flesh, or his fiery amber eyes, but she wept at the scars covering his body. Her eyes washed over the caramel-colored marks of whips, the disfigurement of his chest, and she gasped as she remembered the spot where Dro's knife passed through his shoulder. Yet, there he stood, tall and strong. And just as her arms began to forget the command Ishtar ordered, the woman tossed off her cloak and charged. Alli took one step, and in an instant, Ishtar's wind was swirling gently around her neck. Understanding the threat, she willed herself to stand there and watch.

Brandishing two jagged gold-laced knives the woman was on Narrock in seconds. In a fury of cuts and slashes, she gave him no time to think. Without a second thought, he called forth his hardening and easily deflected every strike she attempted. Stepping back, she released the hidden knife in her boot, and as she kicked him across his temple, the blade shattered into pieces.

"Not bad," she said as she went back on the offensive.

Feigning a superman punch, she immediately went into a leg sweep, thinking she could catch him off guard. She quickly dug her sweeping foot into the ground as Narrock raised his foot to avoid her sweep. Pivoting, she shifted all her body weight into her back leg as she aimed for his unguarded chin. She knew it connected as she saw him catapulted into the air. Not wanting to lose any momentum, she planted her foot and exploded into a moon flip kick. What she had not realized was her first kick did not connect, and as she was about to make contact with Narrock, he flashed a smile as his fist was on a collision course with her face. Before he could connect, he felt a stream of warm liquid roll from his eyebrow down to his cheek, a result of her channeling her wind magic into a blade around her foot.

When he realized what happened, he snapped. Up until now, he had not made any real attempt to fight back, but when she drew blood with her wind, all the rage built up at the hands of Ba'al erupted, and with a blood-curdling roar that shook the very earth, Narrock was on the woman with blinding speed. She had no time to prepare. As her eyes met his, she experienced fear like she never knew before. His eyes burned through her mind. Gone was her will to live, let alone fight. So she waited, and with nothing left to do but close her eyes, she braced for the inevitable blow that carried every ounce of his anger wrapped within every drop of his strength. For the first time, he set his intent on ending this woman, and everyone watching knew. Ishtar raised his hand and right before Narrock's fist connected,

Ishtar grabbed him using his wind. But Ishtar's magic was not enough to stop the inertia of Narrock's punch. While it did not connect, the furiousness of his punch blasted a hole in Ishtar's magic. The reverberation of the blast sent her flying backward to the ground. Ishtar stood there in amazement but kept his face indifferent. While he only placed a little more than a quarter of his strength into his magic, he could feel his wind falter against Narrock's brute strength.

"Very impressive. I must say, you have exceeded my expectation."

Ishtar grabbed him firmly with his wind and vaulted him in the air and slammed him so hard into the ground that the ground cracked. Had Narrock not been using his hardening, the force of the slam would have easily killed him. Yet again, he was reminded of just how helpless he was against this power to control the elements. Ishtar walked over to where he had been embedded into the ground and crouched.

"You know, there are not very many people who could survive that, yet you did. I see that my rennie has been well spent."

Narrock snarled as he was still being held down by Ishtar's magic.

"By the way, the girl you almost killed—that's my

daughter," he said with a playful smile. "Dear, introduce yourself."

"My name is Erridus, daughter of Routen Ishtar," she said as she dusted herself off.

Alli's mouth dropped as she put the final piece in place. The note, the Den, her being excused from servant duties, the woman who threw her in the cage and accompanied her during so many fights was Ishtar's daughter?

"Oh come now Hailey, don't act so surprised. Any idiot should have been able to figure that much out. I mean, it's not like I tried that hard to hide it from you."

"It's quite alright dear. No need to keep her identity a secret from our new friend here," Ishtar said as he flicked his wrist towards Alli, pushing back the hood of her cloak.

Narrock looked up, and all the breath that remained in his body was knocked out of him.

NINETEEN

Hope

66 This has got to be the most ungraceful sight I have ever witnessed in my life," Erridus mused to Alli. "I don't think I have ever seen anyone fall off a horse this much."

She pulled her gaze away from Narrock, whose body continued to fling itself towards the ground with every attempt to mount his stallion.

"How," she hesitated, "how come you didn't tell me sooner?"

"Tell you what?" Erridus asked, dancing around the question.

"Why didn't you just tell me you were Ishtar's daughter from the beginning?"

"Would it have made any difference?"

"Yes! No. I don't know. Maybe. It just would have been nice to know."

"If I told you, would you have worked as hard to improve your skills?" Shrugging her shoulders, she returned her gaze to Narrock.

"It is rather amusing."

Erridus moved her horse closer to her and whispered, "I wanted you to be able to at least stand next to him." Then she rode over to yell at Narrock, "You have got to be the most incompetent and uncoordinated man I have ever met!"

For ten years, she wondered if she would ever see him again, and now, there he was. The boy she always watched from the moment he entered her camp. The boy who would do everything he could to protect them. The boy whose arms she rested in, staring into his...and with that, she had been dropped back into the present just like she had fallen to the ground that day. But she smiled, and as she did, a single tear caressed her cheek as it fell. She finally allowed herself to feel what she forced down since the moment Ishtar ignited hope in her, and she was grateful.

"You blubbering idiot, it's not that hard to mount a horse!" Erridus yelled as she moved toward Narrock.

And for the first time, in a very long time, Alli laughed from the soul of her existence.

TWENTY

A Warrior Mourns

Ishtar made the decision to forgo the coach and travel by horse the day before they were to depart. He wanted to use this as an opportunity to learn more about the fighter he now owned. After they wasted nearly half a day teaching Narrock to ride, they finally began their journey back to Valencia-Cardinal. Narrock could not believe his eyes. All he had known for the past decade was the confines of the Coliseum in Valencia–Parish, and now he found himself much like Alli on her journey. As he rode, his eyes flicked from flower to tree, lake to bird, beast to valley, and finally to Alli. She had since removed her traveler's cloak and was now wearing her riding clothes. He gazed at the richness of her honeyed skin. He could see the soft bruising that still rested on her face which left him wondering where and when she had received them. He followed her hair swaying in the wind. He watched as the wind intertwined with the soft fluffiness of her curls and admired the length of her long white tendrils with splashes of plum highlights. As the wind danced in her hair, it revealed the nape of her neck. He began fawning as his amber eyes brushed down along her delicate shoulders to watch as her bodice delicately held the ample pleasure of her breast so close. While he could not see all of what was contained within, he could tell she had a lake he so desperately wanted to dive into. He started to imagine his arms around her trim waist, and as if she could feel his fondling eyes, Alli turned her head ever so slightly until their eyes met and held. The next thing he knew, Narrock once again went tumbling to the ground.

"Perhaps you should focus your attention on your horse. I'm sure it would help to keep you balanced," Ishtar said, gesturing his head towards the male. "Now, if you don't mind fixing yourself, I would like to make good use of the remaining light we have after wasting the better part of the day teaching you to stay erect." As an extra jab, he added, "And I don't mean in your current state."

"Jealous?" Erridus said.

Narrock glanced her way. Both their feminine faces

looked as if they had been dusted to emulate red berries. He followed their gaze downward to see what Ishtar meant. He looked both women dead in the eye, flashed an unapologetic smirk, and returned to his horse. He did not miss the male's disgust as his eyes rolled and he sauntered off.

Breaking the tree line, Narrock's eyes widened in amazement at what he saw. Dismounting his horse, he walked to the ridgeline, and when Alli turned to behold him, he did not care if she, or anybody here, saw the tears flowing down his face, feeding the winding river separating Valencia–Commonwealth and Valencia-Cardinal. He watched the sky begin to dim in the warm setting, the light of fire blazing as the sun laid to rest behind the Cathedral Mountains. While the others tethered the horses and established camp, Narrock stood there as if reborn a tree. When the sun had set, he watched as the goddess of the night took her place in the celestials, and he bathed in the light of every star that studded the sea of midnight blue, all the while his own tears pooling at his feet. It was the first time he beheld the beauty of this world, and it was the first time he mourned for his world, as well as the loss of his kin.

It had been a while since Alli left him standing on the ridge. She took up her duties preparing the evening meal and tending to the horses. Their party was only seven members.

There was Ishtar, his daughter, one Shadow, and three Toultyn. Narrock increased their party to eight, but there were more than enough provisions to account for the additional member. When Alli signaled that their meal was ready, everyone except Narrock scurried over to the fireside to eat. Ishtar took his serving first, even though he waited for everyone else to be served before he started eating. They ate in silence. Everyone occasionally glancing Narrock's way wondering when he would join them. When everyone had eaten, and Narrock still stood along the ridgeline, Alli took care to set his portion aside as she cleaned up. Lost in her thoughts, she jumped when she noticed Ishtar standing silently right beside her.

"What is wrong with your friend? He hasn't moved since we got here."

Alli shook her head. Holding back her own tears, she was unable to provide a response. Truthfully, even though she pined for him when they were younger, she had to admit she really did not know much about him then, and she probably knew even less about him now.

"Should I be concerned?" Ishtar raised his brow while pretending to pick at the dirt in his nails.

"Narrock is a protector. He won't do anything that would put me in danger."

"Tell me something," he said, closing the gap between them. "Should I be worried about you?" he asked as he gently tucked a stray lock behind her ear.

As he did, he allowed his fingers to softly trace her jawline before brushing away the tear that formed. She took a deep breath at his touch. When she did, she inhaled his peppered wood aroma, and it made her knees buckle. She was surprised by how soft his callus covered hand felt against her skin. Desire. As if their being in nature had awoken some primal desire, she wanted him. Right now, under the star-lit sky.

"I'm fine," she told him. Even though she definitely was not.

Since the first time Ishtar summoned her, she found herself desperately wanting to taste the touch of his lips against hers, but the conflict she now faced condemned her. There Narrock stood. These people enslaved him and forced him to fight for his life for ten long years. These strangers killed her master and stole her kindred. They did not stop there. No, they stole their lives away. For three years, they systematically destroyed the fabric of their culture, and replaced it with theirs through the indoctrination course. Forced them into servitude, and she should hate them. For seven years, she and Ionis constantly reminded themselves who they were. They practiced in secret to fuel their defiance, and now, the warrior she pined for stood mourning while the captor she should hate touched her in a way she desperately wanted more of.

"Allister, what is it that you feel for that male?" She watched as Ishtar's eyes passed from her to Narrock and back to her.

"Narrock is like a brother to me."

She cursed herself for the lie that crossed her lips as she brushed at invisible dust on her thighs. She knew she felt more for him, but she also did not want to put him in any danger.

"Good," was all he said, letting silence draw a line in the ground. "There was something else I wanted to talk to you about," he said, slightly shifting the conversation. "About that day," he combed his hand through his hair, lingering at the back, his stare drifting heavenward. "I am sorry for what Dendaron and Brista tried to do to you."

With those words, the memories of that day came rushing back. The face of her attacker whose tongue laid on the floor. Brista's scream silenced by the blade lodge in her throat. Ishtar's graze across her thighs, the sensation of his breath warming her cheeks, and the way that man's head exploded like a ripe melon in his hand.

"Thank you," she said, trying to hide her mixed fear and desire of the Routen.

"That is why I have decided that when we return, you will share my quarters."

Surprise shattered her mask of indifference. "My lord, I don't think that—"

"I never asked you to think. As the Routen, I am responsible for the welfare of all who reside in my house. This is my order, and 'no' is not an option offered to you. Do you understand?" As he touched her chin again, he allowed his silver frost dusted eyes to dive deep into her soul. Then, once again looking to Narrock. "Ensure he understands as well." He turned for his tent.

"It seems my father has taken a liking to you, Ms. Allister," Alli let out a soft shriek as Erridus stepped out of the brush.

"Were you spying on us?"

"On the contrary, I was simply using the ladies' bush." At this, both girls chuckled. "I will only offer you this warning. Your friend's life is in your hands. His death will either come in the tournament or as a result of you," she said with no trace of the humor before heading toward her tent. "Oh, and Allister," she stopped, her eyes connecting with hers, "I can see why you have grown on my father." She shared a brief smile and disappeared into the night.

After she finished putting everything away, Alli wordlessly

took her place along Narrock.

"For ten years, every day, I have watched as everyone die before me. I have buried those feelings so far down not even the sun could reach them." He spoke in their native tongue with so many outsiders around. She could feel a knot developing in her throat as she listened. "And then, I saw you." He turned to her. She could see where the salt from his tears stained his face. As she reached up to touch his face, he grasped her wrist. "Tell me, how do you feel after opening your legs to the people who killed our family?"

Instantly, her eyes glassed over at the cut Narrock's words delivered. Yanking her hand free, she slapped him across his face.

"How dare you say that to me? I can't believe that after all this time dreaming of what it would feel like to see you that these are your first words to me!" Turning on her heels, She took three steps toward her tent before she stopped. "And for your information," turning on him, hellfire blazing in her eyes, "you know, you have no right to judge me. But if that is what you want to think of me, then so be it. But let me tell you something Narrock. You are not the only one who has fought to survive."

TWENTY-ONE

The Lokia

Alli woke the next morning with the same anger she went to sleep with. She could not understand why so many people were taking an interest in what males she never even slept with. And even though the chill in the air sent shivers through her body, she felt nothing. Opening the flap to her tent, she suddenly found herself forgetting why she was so upset. There, sitting with his back to her tent, was Narrock. The sight of the dew on his torn pants, barely holding together, told her he had been there a while. That, along with the loss of color from his deep rich skin.

She just stood there, arms crossed, trying and failing to find something to say.

"I was wrong, and I'm sorry," he said without turning around.

"I suppose you figured if you waited here long enough I would have to speak to you, is that it?"

"No."

"Then why are you doing this?"

At this point, he stood and faced her. "Because I will always protect you." Then he turned and walked away.

Instead of evaporating, the single tear that slid down her face froze. Realization set in. He had been sitting there guarding her. Once again, he left her speechless. *Why*, she thought, *why is he always protecting me?* Pushing the question from her thoughts, she brushed the frozen tear from her cheek and began her duty of preparing the morning meal.

When the rest of the party had risen for the day, Alli excused herself into the trees while everyone else ate. The frenzy of emotions she was experiencing left her unnerved, and she felt she just needed to get away. She had been so distracted in her feelings that she did not notice she was being stalked. When the pains in her chest finally paralyzed her legs, the weight of her body collapsed to the flower-covered ground, and she heard it before she saw it.

As the massive creature emerged from the brush, a twig snapped underneath its powerful and unforgiving paw. Alli looked up and was staring in the face of an inferno. The beast breathed steam from its muzzle and slowly drew back its lips to reveal a row of razor-sharp teeth and canines capable of piercing steel. As it stood there, she choked down a scream frantic to get out. She knew at this moment the best thing would be to calm herself and hope it would walk away. But it did not. It continued to stalk forward. Each step crackled in the chilled air until she realized the steam rising from his paws and gasped in horror as its claws scorched the earth. Without warning, it pounced.

Alli's scream was answered as Narrock barreled his shoulder into the beast. It crashed against a tree, instantly incinerating it to ash. The two predators stood, fires blazing in their eyes, the roar of the creature was met with Narrock's war cry. They charged. he dodged the first swipe of its claws, but the second connected drawing blood and sending him through several trees before he finally collided with a giant boulder. His vision blurred from the impact and loss of blood from the gash across his arm, but he knew if he did not get up, Alli was going to die. He watched as it turned its attention from him back to Alli. It started after its original prey. Freeing himself from the boulder, Narrock shattered the stone in two and hurled it towards the beast. It easily dodged his first and second throw, but his intention was not to hit it with the rock. As it was distracted, Narrock placed all his might into a devastating blow and planted his fist right between the creature's eyes. Bone cracked, and the beast reared back on its hind legs writhing in pain. But when it came down, its fangs cleaved through his shoulder.

He saw it coming, but his hardening was no match for the creature's teeth sinking through his flesh and into his bone like they were wet clay. Narrock's blood-curdling scream shook the ground rupturing the beast's ears as it let go and pawed at its ears. Locking eyes with Alli, the creature took one step before twitching its ears and darting back into the trees. Just as it disappeared, Ishtar, his men, and Erridus burst through the trees.

"Capture that Fire Lokia! I want it alive!" he commanded his Shadow. They nodded before chasing after the creature.

"Father!" Erridus cried.

Alli was beside herself as she hysterically fumbled over Narrock's body, her tears washing the blood from his wounds. Ishtar and Erridus rush to his side, Erridus dragging Alli away.

Using his wind, Ishtar enveloped him to slow his breathing and prevent further contamination. Tapping into the healing ability of stonebreaker magic, he encased him in earth and began stitching his shoulder back into place.

"Erridus, prepare the horses, we leave now!"

With quickness, Erridus took Alli with her to pack everything and prepare to leave.

"My father's stonebreaker magic will bind his shoulder, but he will need to get to the healers quickly if he is to live," she said to Alli.

In a flash, the two women packed only what was necessary and were on their way back to Ishtar. It took some engineering, but eventually, he found a way to connect the cocooned Narrock to his horse, and they were dashing through the woods.

"What was that thing?!" Alli shouted over the thunder of the horses.

"It's called a Lokia," Erridus answered. "That one was fire-based."

"Fire-based?"

"Yes, they are magical creatures capable of ultimate destruction. We were lucky there was no fire around."

"I don't understand."

"That one feeds on fire."

"Water, wind, earth, they are the guardians, and we were lucky. Now, shut up and let me concentrate," Ishtar said as they went barreling for the nearest healers' convent.

TWENTY-TWO

Inderrah

Narrock's eyes fluttered open and immediately his hand shot to his shoulder. What the...There was no bite, and he struggled to comprehend why there was not a pool of blood where he observed. As he looked around, his chest tightened, constricting his airways. The rhythmic cadence of his heart skyrocketed. Pushing off the ground, he turned to survey his surroundings and to gather his bearings. He could not comprehend what was happening. The last thing he remembered were the teeth of some creature born of an inferno slicing through his flesh, and now he was on top a mountain. The dense fog seemed to cascade off the ridges forming an ocean of clouds that swallowed his vision, save for the sun as it retreated toward its resting place.

"Guess this means I'm dead."

"Young Jazwon, I assure you, you are not dead."

Narrock whirled around, eyes wide open in alarm as standing before him was a warrior. He wore the cloth of the Gwhin, the fearless warriors of Jhatar sworn to protect their leader, the K'ron. The distinct cinnamon striping set across the honeycomb and white hide around his waist suggested his inteszar was made of the fur from the sabered huntress. And the intricate craftsmanship of his charcoal rose metal soarre shine as it clung to his forearms and calves. Narrock was reminded of his father. For the Jazwon, these were earned only after unlocking all five upper limits and being excepted into an elite training covenant. The male before him was taller than Narrock, a pillar of forged steel contained in the same rich sienna that cloaked him. Carved all along his body were the stories of his conquest. The legends of victory.

"I don't understand. If I'm not dead, then where am I?"

"You are at the entrance to the Temple of Inderrah."

His brow furrowed. *The Temple of Inderrah is on Jhatar*, he thought.

Inderrah was the temple where those permitted to journey released their spiritual limits. Narrock had already released his physical and emotional limits, but he had done so on Jhatar. Those temples were pristine. One made of ivory, the other of onyx. Their exact locations were secret. However, the lands which housed them were guarded by the temple masters. He remembered how alike the temples were. Radiant, sacred, surreal. But this place. How was he expected to believe he was back in his world when the truth screamed he was lying in the forest on Valencia dying?

"You lie."

"I have no such reason to lie to you. You are at the Temple of Inderrah." The male took a step towards him.

"Then tell me, how did I get back to Jhatar?" he asked, taking a step back.

The male paused and studied him for a moment. "Who said anything about Jhatar?"

Narrock opened his mouth to respond, but nothing came out. Finally, he asked, "Then where?"

"I do not like repeating myself. My original statement still stands and will not change at any point. Now, why don't you try saying something of value?" the warrior said clearly annoyed.

Narrock screamed, as the fog around him climbed into

the air, and the male vanished. He slid his hands into his locs and pulled them over his shoulders before interlacing his fingers atop his head. None of this made sense. Composing himself, he turned back in the direction of the warrior. For a moment, he peered through the fog, and then, as if the mist recognized he had indeed cooled off, it pulled back, and the male materialized once again.

"Who are you?"

"My name is Draxtin. I am Jazwon, and I am Gwhin."

Rubbing his hand across his chin, he paused, "Are you dead?"

"Physically, yes."

"Then does this mean I am between life and death?" he held his breath waiting for Draxtin's response.

"In this moment, yes. Your body is still in the physical world while your spirit has traversed here. However, you are not here for judgment."

"Then why am I here?"

"Because it is time for you to break through the limits of your spirit, and I am here to guide you."

As Draxtin spoke these words, understanding seemed to wash over him. He had begun his rite of passage. Immediately,

Narrock bowed pressing his head to the ground. He knew his behavior was not honorable and hoped he would be forgiven. Draxtin waved him to his feet and placed his hand upon his shoulder.

"Young warrior, you have been through many a great trials. I have watched and waited for you to show you were ready. But I feel it is imperative to begin your journey now if you are to overcome your greatest trial."

Narrock turned and walked away until he almost stepped off the edge of the ridge, thanks to the fog that still blotted out his vision. Peering out into the dense white ocean, he watched as the sun settled in the distance casting a cascading burst of oranges, yellows, and reds across the sky. Allowing his resolve to set, he faced Draxtin.

"When do we begin?"

Draxtin turned and walked into the fog. Where before, the low hanging clouds swallowed him, this time a path cleared. A massive cast-iron gate with ruins and grave markings on the other side was revealed. Following Draxtin, he went to cross the threshold when a giant winged red-tail bird dug its talons into his back and chest. Its wings boomed as it lifted into the sky, flying away from the mountain and dropped him into the white ocean now saturated with the colors of the setting sun.

His stomach was in his throat as his body sliced through the air. Unable to breathe, he reached out desperately hoping to grab onto something to stop his descent. When he resigned to his fate, he stopped flailing. Focusing his eyes towards the ground, Narrock prepared. The sound of the air splitting apart from him went silent as the ground rapidly approached, and he cursed as he braced for the impact. Abruptly, he awoke back in the physical world. His lungs expanded beyond their normal capacity that he could feel them ready to burst. Relief came as he release one giant exhale. Several times this repeated until his breathing steadied. As his senses returned, he was suddenly aware of the warm touch of flesh wrapped around his neck and the cool splatter of tears across his face. Then, the pain in his shoulder came racing back, and he blacked out from the overload. His thoughts lost in the intoxicating madness of agony.

TWENTY-THREE

Fire & Wind

It had been a week since Narrock was released from the healing convent. Ishtar sat in his study when he received the report from his Shadows. Before he finished reading, he grabbed the glass of cider and hurled it across the room.

"Don't you think you're being a bit overly dramatic Father?" Erridus lay perched in the window reading from her book.

"Not only did they fail to capture the Fire Lokai, but that creature killed one of my men." Ishtar's shoulders dropped as he buried his face in his hand.

"At least there's good news—"

"Erridus, please. What is good about having the Reinzour sending his dogs to my territory?" This bit of information caught Erridus off guard. Ishtar noticed. "I take it there are some things even you don't know then."

"Sorry, I can't be everywhere all the time."

Sighing heavily, he poured another glass of cider and drank deeply. "First, my fighter almost dies. Then I lose the Fire Lokai, and now this."

"Well, like I said, at least there is some good news." Ishtar flashed her an annoyed look. "I guess you don't want to hear about the male and his gorgeous eyes, sexy lips, the fact that he will live?"

"How long has he been awake?" he asked rolling his eyes and shaking his head.

"It's been about half a day."

"And you waited until now to tell me?" he questioned rising from his chair and slamming his hands on the desk.

"Somebody needs a nap." He opened his mouth, but she

continued. "I wanted to make sure he would stay awake first. Anyways, you would be happy to know there is virtually no pain left in his shoulder."

"I'm sorry, the letter from the Reinzour flustered me. Have the healers said he can start sparring?" She shook her head.

"They believe it will be at least another week before he can."

He mulled this information over for a moment before downing another glass of cider. "Take me to him."

They entered through a secret passage near the back of Ishtar's study where he kept his favorite exotics from his excursions. The damp smell of mold filled the pathway as they traveled down several flights of stairs. When they reached the landing, they took an immediate right and entered a narrow corridor before stopping in front of the lone wall lantern. Turning toward the opposite wall, they pushed it aside and ascended a flight of stairs before exiting through the secret passage from his private examination room into the healing hall.

Entering the healing hall, he summoned the Chief Healer for a full report. When he had been briefed, he was led down the corridor to the last room on the left. This chamber, generally reserved for his personal Shadows, had been sanctioned for Narrock considering how important he was at the moment. When they entered the room, Narrock was sitting on the bed, legs hanging off the sides with his elbows braced firmly on his thighs. Slowly, he raised his gaze to meet Ishtar's and the inaudible pissing contest bathed the room in dark tension.

"If you two are done jocking for the biggest..." Erridus added an extra gesture for fun, "then can we please be done with this egotistical display of male dominance?" Ishtar shot her a cutting look. "What? I'm just saying we didn't come down here for you two to cross swords."

Narrock released a soft rumbling laugh that erupted into roaring laughter so intense, he felt the stitching in his shoulder strain.

"Now this one I like," he said, wiping the tear from his eye.

"Glad you find me amusing," she said, the corner of her lips curving upward, teasing of devilish intention.

Taking a seat across from him, the Routen cleared his throat and tried to regain control in the room. "Tell me what happened with the Fire Lokai."

"The Fire what?"

"Listen here, *boy*—"

"Do not, call me, boy." Narrock said to Ishtar. In a predatorial whisper.

"You will be whoever I say you are." There was a loud crack as the chair shattered upon impacting with the wall.

Narrock straightened his back, returning his elbows to his lap, defiance setting his amber eyes ablaze. "No, I won't." Then he rolled back his shoulders, displaying the scar running across his chest.

"Is that a challenge?" Ishtar said, powerful currents swirling around him.

Narrock balked at the wind. "Is this a cha—"

Before the words could finish leaving his lips, the Routen grabbed him by his collar, whirled him around, and slammed him into the wall. Allowing his anger to get the best of him, Ishtar drove his white-knuckled fist into Narrock's rib-cage, shattering his bones. The male coughed up blood and bared his teeth. Surprised, he glanced down to see Narrock caught his punch, despite breaking his bones.

Narrock refused to yield one inch, even though he realized something was wrong. Both males' attention was fractured as Erridus applauded.

"Congratulations, you are both...Nevermind."

When he released his magic and separated his fist from Narrock's ribs, he regrettably started counting the cost of answering the male's provocation. Though he did not show it, he knew he just set back the fighter's recovery, and the Reinzour's Shadow would be here in a few days. The chief healer quietly replaced the destroyed chair, and Ishtar sat with an arrogant display of nobility.

"Sit."

Narrock forbade his body to speak the truth of the immense pain he felt. Instead, he forced it into submission as he walked to his bed, every muscle protesting the movement. He demanded his breathing to steady as he willed every ounce of pain to vacate his body.

"Will you tell me about your scars?" Erridus inquired curiously.

She hoped this would help placate the tension in the air. After a moment, Narrock allowed his eyes to wander to her. She was beautiful. Her gentle frame was like a white canvas painted with the elegance of her features. Her cheeks sat upon a high throne with her ruby eyes promising the sensual soothing of the sea. The lines of her face sang of sophisticated grace, and were framed by the beautiful phoenix-fire hanging in a loose braid down her back.

"A guard thought he could steal my essence. He was wrong." When speaking to her, his posture softened, if only a little.

"They called you Derrius when we came to see you. If that is not your name, will you tell us what is?" Despite the explosive nature of their first meeting, Narrock was finding himself drawn to her. The attention and care she displayed slowly disarmed him.

"I have inherited the name Narrock from my people."

"And you were given the name Derrius by ours." Ishtar was losing his patience with the song and dance. Noticing, Narrock leaned back and laughed. "I don't see what's so funny."

"The guard said the same thing," his laugh died, and his expression cleared. "His death came with my refusal to accept it."

"You arrogant little—"

"Father, your cause is tied to his success. Maybe you should not disregard him." This drew ire from Ishtar, but she did not care. Her job was to assist her father, and clearly, he was failing. "Narrock, will you fight for us in this tournament?"

He scoffed. "You attack me. Dishonor me. Yet, you expect me to fight." She turned her attention to Ishtar before looking back, her eyes speaking condemnation. "I have no reason to fight, not for you."

Ishtar lashed out, "You have no reason you say. I will kill you where you sit, is that reason enough for you?"

Resting his shoulders against the wall, "I've been dead since I was brought to this world."

The walls began to groan and splinter, a clear sign of Ishtar losing his temper.

"Your threats mean nothing to me."

"If not for us, then what will you fight for?" she jumped in before her father actually killed him.

His eyes twitched as his head turned to the side. "You hold me against my will and demand I fight for you to achieve glory with your ruler." He paused to let that settle in and considered his next words carefully. "I refuse to fight for you. I fight for my freedom and the freedom of my kindred."

Ishtar's jaw grated at his outlandish request. Erridus leaned over and whispered something in her father's ear. Narrock's honed hearing allowed him to listen easily without detection.

They have no idea what I am capable of, he thought to himself.

"*Fine*. I will promise you and your kindred freedom. Do you have any other demands?"

"Freedom on *my* world."

Ishtar glared at him, his hands digging deep into the chair. "Fine," he said through clenched teeth. This brought a smile to Narrock's face. "My terms are simple. Win, and I will do everything in my power to see your request through. However,"—pausing for dramatic effect—"if you fail to win, I will boil the one you call Ionis in silver. I will cut your eyelids off. Hang you from the ceiling, and make you watch as I kill Allister in the most cruel and unimaginable way possible. And afterward. I will see to your slow and miserable death." Heat began to emanate from Narrock. "Oh," he said as he stood to leave, "the girl's life will be snatched at any point you get out of control." Ishtar departed while Erridus stayed.

"Narrock, thank you. My father is not a cruel man. Honor is his currency."

When she left, the world came crashing down on him and sent him into a convulsive pit of darkness.

TWENTY-FOUR

Kill the Messenger

Today was the eighth day the heavens cried such sorrowful tears. It had been years since the last time Ishtar's house experienced this kind of torrential downpour. As the rain pounded upon the earth, the structure of the ridges and land began to give way. The massive landslides carry people and houses with it.

"Don't stop! Their lives depend on you," shouted Ishtar's top Shadows to the lower ranking Toultyn.

The vortex-dancers fought desperately to slow the current of the streams while stonebreakers did their best to direct the mass of oozing clay away from populated ones into empty areas. Water and earth, both doing all they could to save as many lives as possible.

She watched from her chambers as all non-magic and weaker users were instructed to stay inside. The sight was ghastly. Land shifting and sharpening like it was on a pottery wheel. She could not shake the feeling of helplessness. This may not be her home, but it became her placeholder. Just then, a giant boom rattled the area, unleashing a nest of angry serpents that recoiled just as fast as they attacked. Alli felt as if the entire world came to a stand-still. She watched in horror when not a serpent, but a dragon stepped through the clouds. It pulsated in radiant lights, indiscriminately striking the ground and setting fires everywhere it touched. Its head peered around looking for prey, and when it locked its eyes, made of pure light, on her, it gathered all of its luminance into its stomach. Twisting its neck, the dragon's head snapped forward, jaws wide as focused beams of blue light erupted from its mouth. The mixture of flashes and its roars left everyone blinded and deaf, and Alli in darkness.

She found herself back on Jhatar, this time in the

infirmary. She could hear people talking. Focusing her ears in their direction, she listened.

"I don't understand. She's just a child," a woman's voice said. It was oddly familiar, but she could not quite place it. Another spoke, this one hoarse as if they had been screaming.

"I told you, it is unnatural how unlucky this girl is."

The next voice she knew. It was Master Centrine. "Her gifting is too strong."

"We have never seen a child so young release their spiritual limit," the female voice said.

"And she has no control," the hoarse voice spoke.

They continued like this until Master Centrine silenced them. "It pains me, but we have to close her limit."

"It's too dangerous," the woman said.

"It's more dangerous to leave them unchecked." The amount of pain in Master Centrine's voice sent shivers down Alli's bones.

"She may never be able to release her limits if we do this."

Though his voice was harsh, there was a tenderness about it the way he spoke. Alli's attention was broken when she noticed cold drops of water landing on her skin. As the rain started to flow, she lifted her head toward the sky and pressed herself hard against the wall, all the breath in her lungs lost. Her sapphire eyes accented with the electric pulse before her. There, staring back at her, was the dragon. And without warning, it struck.

Alli woke in the healing hall. Her eyes fluttered open. Her clothes were damp as they clung to her. She sat up and buried her face in her hands.

"I see you've finally decided to wake up." Erridus was sitting in the chair by her bedside.

"How long have I been asleep?" Allie asked rubbing her forehead.

"Let see, it's been a day since we found you."

"Found me?" she asked, lifting a brow.

Erridus went on to explain how a giant bolt of lightning broke through the sky and ended the torrential downpour. When the clouds dissipated, the sun stood proudly at the height of its summit. Erridus continued, explaining how they searched to find survivors and circled back to survey the damage from the lightning that struck the house.

"When we checked on the servants, we found you in your room unconscious, with scorch marks splintered along the walls."

Then, as if her foggy mind was jolted back to focus, she remembered the moment right before the pulsing dragon attacked. The memory triggered the terror she felt at that moment. Out of nowhere, she began to scream and flail around as if this time, the attack was slow and deliberate. Suddenly, the door to the chamber exploded from where it was cinched into the wall, and Narrock barreled through. He locked eyes on Alli and then shot a deathly stare at Erridus. Without a second thought, he rushed to Alli and gathered her in his arms. The warmth of his embrace, along with the rhythmic dance of his heart, eased her back to herself.

"You called?" a voice asked in the distance.

Alli felt her body slightly thrown back, hands gripping her shoulders tight. When she looked up, her heart cracked at the look of pure disgust in Narrock's face. Tears formed at the base of her eyes. Allowing her glance to travel to where the other voice came from. Abruptly, she was aware of Ishtar standing in the doorway where a splinter of the door was still attached to the hinges. Then she understood her mistake. Narrock rushed in while she was panicking, but instead of calling his name, she called Ishtar's.

Narrock pulled his eyes from hers, and she was again reminded of the time he coldly dropped her to the floor as a child. Guilt flowed through her. He nearly died saving her

154

twice, and even now, he showed up to protect her. Yet, again she found herself choosing her master over her kin. She reached for him. An apology stuck in her throat. But before she could reach him, her hand returned to her side. Ishtar watched, intrigued by what was happening. She felt Ishtar's assessing stare and remembered her claim that Narrock was like a brother. She stopped. Stopped feeling and ignored the ache she felt with each heartbeat. Narrock protected her, and now, it was her turn to do the same. So she bit her tongue and watched him silently make his way to the door.

"Narrock?" Erridus called to him. "As you see, she is well." The slight bob of his head was enough for her to know his decision.

"Ensure he is fully recovered in three days," Ishtar said turning to the Chief Healer who was standing in the corridor.

"Yes, your lordship."

Without a word, Narrock followed the healer and disappeared into the darkness of the candle-lit hallway.

"He seems smitten by you." Erridus said.

Alli shook her head. "No. He has always viewed himself as a protector."

"He has agreed to be my representative," Ishtar said. She said nothing, still sensing his assessing gaze. "The condition, however, is that no harm comes to you. So imagine how I felt to have my word broken so quickly." Something tightened in her chest as her her eyes met his, unable to understand his intent. "Do try not to die on me again Allister. I quite like having you around." He flashed a sensual smile before leaving.

He did not know why, but recalling what just happened brought Ishtar blissful happiness. Alli cradled in Narrock's arm while she called his name. At the same time, it caused him significant discomfort. He was the Head of the House, and yet, somehow, he started to have these feelings for a servant girl not even from his world. As his internal debate continued, he was suddenly reminded of his conversation with Allister on the road back. In the sequence of events, he had forgotten he was going to have her transferred to his chambers. Fatigue started to set in, and he let out a heavy sigh. When he exited the stairwell into the main hall, he was greeted by one of his Shadows.

"Sir, Reynuck of the Reinzour's personal Shadow has arrived and is waiting for you in your receiving hall."

Ishtar found himself wanting to pound his head through the wall, but he simply sighed and dismissed his Shadow. When he arrived at the hall, it took everything in him from sending a slicing wind-blade at the young guard.

"Kindly remove yourself from my chair," his voice carried a genuine threat of death.

The hall was massive. Long red velvet tapestry hung from the tall cathedral walls, bearing the scarlet feather honed into a blade on the current of wind, the Ishtar household crest. An ornate carpet connected the entryway to the Head's chair sitting atop twelve steps laid with gold, each a tribute to the former Heads dating back to before their arrival on this planet. Each told the tale of their conquest and rule. In the massive chair carved from onyx inlaid with emeralds, amethysts, and rubies with white gold trimming, sat Reynuck.

"Now, is that any way to speak to the Reinzour's personal Shadow?" sarcasm bathing his words.

"You would dare to disrespect one of his commanders in their own house," he said through gritted teeth.

"Perhaps I shouldn't have been made to wait."

Ishtar found himself releasing a hearty laugh that echoed through the hall. When his laughter died, it felt as if all the air in the room began migrating to him. And in a violent eruption, his magic swelled filling the room with a wind force capable of complete and utter destruction. Reynuck's eyes widened in pure terror. His back stiffened and his fingers clung desperately to the arms of the throne. Ishtar was the most distinguished of the tempest-kissed, and his mastery was of full display as his wind rendered Reynuck's dragon-spawned abilities none-existent. The oxygen around Reynuck had been stripped, leaving him unable to ignite any fire. His mouth dropped open and his heart beat so hard in his chest he thought it would burst. If things were not already bad enough, he gasped in horror as a noble-winged creature materialized in the angry cyclone. Its razor-sharp beak and talons poised to kill. As Reynuck's gaze connected with his dominate stare, the young guard bowed placing one knee on the ground with his opposite fist and dipped his chin deep, signaling a request for mercy.

Ishtar, now hovering over Reynuck, reached down placing his hand around his neck to raise his face to his. His fingers gripped so tight that bruises manifested against his pale skin. He leaned forward until Reynuck could see nothing more than the raging torrent thrashing in his dark, cold blue eyes.

"This day you will know your place. And if you ever disrespect me again," he paused allowing the severity of his words to sink in, "I will kill you myself in front of the Reinzour."

Reynuck nodded in compliance and Ishtar's wind vanished. Immediately the servants entered and began putting everything back in its place. The massive hall, meant for entertainment, was drowned in silence before the echoes of clapping hands shattered it.

Erridus stood in the doorway, her slow clap changing tempo. "Bravo, bravo" she cheered mockingly at Reynuck. "Someone, please get him a change of clothes. I think he may have soiled himself."

Embarrassment flooded his face as he became aware of the now cooling dampness of his legs. Ishtar, suddenly aware of it too, looked down and laughed before walking off.

"Bring him to my study after he has had a chance to clean himself up."

Reynuck swore under his breath as Veronica led him to the guest servant's quarters. He had never been so humiliated in his life. How had it turned out this way? As she left, the other male erupted into a fit of laughter. Reynuck glared at him.

"I told you to mind your place when we got here." Reynuck stood and ripped off his shirt before he turned to him. "Before you think to do something stupid remember I am your superior, and I will not hold back like Routen Ishtar just did."

The heaviness filling the room was dark and heavy. Eventually, Reynuck resigned himself to the washroom while Joris continued making jokes. At Ishtar's command, the tub was filled with ice cold water, a reminder to the young guard of his place within this house. Reynuck sneered at this gesture and allowed the heat of his anger to fuel the fire permeating from his pores. In a matter of seconds, he was sitting in a hot tub. After a few moments passed, Joris entered and took a seat.

"Listen, just because you are the Reinzour's Shadow does not mean your status is above the Routen. What happened to you today was mercy. The Reinzour would have executed you on the spot. Remember that."

Reynuck lowered himself deeper into the water, so only his eyes remained afloat. Joris waited until he raised his head to discuss the reason they had come. When they finished, he left the room and prepared for what was to come.

When Ionis returned, she led both officers to Ishtar's study. When they entered, Ishtar was sitting at his desk with Erridus behind him, and Narrock sitting in one of the chairs adjacent from his desk. Joris took the remaining seat with Reynuck standing behind him as was discussed. Neither spoke as they waited for the Routen to address them.

"Why are you here?" he asked.

"Routen Ishtar, we have come on behalf of the Reinzour. His eminence heard about the attack and wanted us to inspect your fighter to determine if the tournament would be delayed."

Ishtar tilted his head slightly to the side. When they said

no more, Erridus leaned forward and whispered something in her father's ear.

As no one seemed to acknowledge Narrock, he took the liberty to listen to what she whispered. Her message was simple, take the delay and paint Narrock as needing the time. This did not sit well with the warrior. While in the Coliseum, weakness was never a word associated with him. He spoke before either of them could answer.

"I am ready to fight."

His statement earned him a deadly glare from Ishtar, but the look of bewilderment was worth it.

"Ignore him."

For the first time, Reynuck looked at the fighter and recognition kicked in. This was the slave he killed two guards for.

"*You!*" he said, pointing his finger.

As Narrock turned his attention to Reynuck, "You're the fire user," he said. "Tell me, why can't I still see you clearly?"

Ishtar and Erridus looked at each other in confusion.

"I don't know what you mean," Reynuck turned his head away in an attempt to dodge the question.

"Yes, you do. Both times I have seen you, a haze has

covered you. Why?" Narrock stood and took a step towards him.

"Enough of this foolishness, we did not come to talk to you."

Ishtar did not miss his desperate attempt to evade the question.

"How do you know my representative?" Ishtar questioned.

"Sir, perhaps that can wait until we have completed the Reinzour's business," Joris said lowering his head.

Ishtar considered this for a moment before repeating his question to him.

Assuming the calm demeanor required to be a covert operative for the Reinzour, he composed himself and recounted the events of the day he encountered the slave. When he finished, he stood there as Ishtar leaned back in his chair.

"Is the Reinzour aware of this?"

Reynuck shock his head. "At the time, he made a full recovery before the auction. There was no need to worry him."

This revelation sparked something inside Ishtar. If Narrock recovered from that beating then surely he would be ready.

"You still have not explained your appearance," Narrock

said wearily watching the guard.

Reynuck resolved not to respond. However, when Ishtar asked him about it, panic ran under the surface. No one had ever realized the concealment magic he used. It was the main reason he had been elected to the personal guard. He served as the Reinzour's spy and assassin carrying out covert missions with no one the wiser. He swore.

"If you wish to keep your tongue, you would do best to mind your language," a steely-eyed Ishtar spoke.

"My apologies, sir. Unfortunately, I am unable to speak of this nature as it is a deep secret of the Reinzour."

Ishtar did not like the answer, but resigned to accept it. "Well, guess that will do." Turning to Narrock, his silent command was understood. Sit down and shut up. Narrock returned to his seat but refused to take his eyes off Reynuck.

"If that is all, tell the Reinzour we would like a two-week delay to make up for the recovery period for my fighter."

Joris bowed his head in understanding. "Commander Ishtar, there is one more thing. The Reinzour has ordered his Shadow Reynuck to remain in your house until the tournament."

Ishtar checked the fury flaring inside as Joris removed the sealed letter from his coat and handed it to him. After reading the letter, Ishtar's jaw tightened.

"Erridus, please show our *guest*...to his chamber."

TWENTY-FIVE

Sisters

Alli had hoped Ishtar was not serious, so when she received the news she was to share his chamber starting today, she did not know what to do. Lost in her thoughts walking down the corridor, she found herself walking past her room all the way to the end and knocked on Ionis' door.

"Oh, look who finally remembered I'm alive." Ionis opened the door but blocked her from entering.

"What are you talking about?" a small crack rippled

through her chest.

"Don't play stupid. You could have at least told me you didn't want to be around me anymore. No, you just let me walk around here thinking it was something I did, but you know what? You are no better than the rest of these bastards!" Ionis went to throw the door shut, but Alli stuck her hand out.

"That's not true," but even as she listened, she knew the truth. "I'm sorry Ionis. I know I haven't been that good a friend lately."

"I don't care! You left me."

"Please, I have nowhere else to go and no one else to talk to."

Ionis considered for a moment before walking away from the door and taking a seat on her bed. Alli walked in and rested her back against the door. She made several attempts to speak, but Ionis' words continued to play in her mind. *You left me.*

"Either start talking or get out."

"I've been training at a place called the Den."

She took a deep breath and told Ionis everything. She watched her friend as she recounted her fights, her second encounter with Ishtar, the Lokia.

"Narrock has agreed to fight, but only for our freedom."

"You're telling me he's in this house right now and you're just now telling me?"

"I'm sorry I didn't tell you as soon as we returned and that I didn't ask if you could come when we left. But now I'm supposed to share a room with Ishtar because of—"

"Spare me your sexcapades." Ionis was clenching her skirts between her fisted hands. "It's okay. Clearly, you are the Routen's favorite. Now, if you would excuse me, I need to get ready." Ionis rose and made her way towards her closet.

"I didn't ask for any of this," she said, throwing her hands in her lap in frustration.

"You never do you selfish bitch."

"Why are you pushing me away?" she grabbed Ionis by her arm and swung her around.

"I didn't push you away. You just left me. You went to this Den thing and didn't even think about taking me. Why?" She jammed her palm into Alli's shoulder. "You went to get Narrock and didn't think about me. Why?" Another strike. "All this time I thought we were in this together." The next strike sent Alli toppling to the floor.

Alli pushed herself up only to be met with tears flooding down Ionis' face. "That's not true!"

"It is, and you know it. This is the first time you've talked to me in weeks! Face it Alli. You've become one of them and I don't matter anymore."

"Ionis, please! That's not true."

She searched her friend, desperate to find the bond they had shared since being brought to this place. But Ionis' stony exterior only carried hurt and anger. Tears began to dot Alli's eyes.

"I'm sorry," she repeated.

"That's the problem. You're always sorry. Well, I'm done trying to be there for you when all you do is leave me behind."

"Ionis, don't do this. I should have told you about the Den sooner, and I should have told you about Narrock. We can go together. I'll take you to Narrock, and we can go to the Den together, and we can both continue to become stronger."

"No." Ionis' face was stone-cold. "I thought you wanted to become stronger together, but you have clearly shown you want to become stronger yourself. I think it is time for you to go be with your new family," she said, wiping the tears from her eyes.

"Ionis, please, you're my sister and I need you."

Ionis simply walked to the door and opened it without a word. "I'm not your sister. Maybe if I was, you would have taken me with you."

Alli pressed her lips together tightly to prevent the sob building in her chest from escaping as she heard the door click softly behind her. When she walked a little ways down the corridor, her body crashed into the wall. The weight from what just happened forced her to the ground. No matter how hard she tried, Alli could not stop the tear in her heart from ripping as she buried her face in her hands and wept.

TWENTY-SIX

Waterfall Garden

Ishtar finished discussing with Erridus his plans to keep Narrock under constant treatment over the next three days in hopes of a complete recovery. He wanted to ensure his fighter was ready to start training immediately afterward, and they wanted to make sure Reynuck was limited in what he was to report. As they parted ways, his eyes fell upon Allister aimlessly wondering about.

"My dear Allister, you're far too pretty to wear that face," he flashed her a warm smile.

"Lord Ishtar. I was just on my way to—"

"See me, I hope. Especially, as I was on my way to see

you."

He watched heat pockets blossom on her cheeks as she averted her gaze to the floor.

"Well, no. I was actually on my way to find Narrock."

"Oh, I'm sorry to hear that." He pressed his lips tight and furrowed his brow. "Unfortunately, you will not be able to see him for a while."

"Is he alright?"

"Your *brother* is fine."

He made sure she did not miss his warning. Again, he wrestled with the conflicting thoughts, the strange desire to have her now, and the calculated side that needed to stick to the plan. He sighed.

"He will be undergoing nonstop treatment until he has completely recovered. I'm not sure how long that will take," he lied.

Ishtar already knew he was going to keep the two separated for as long as he could. He did not need her complicating things more than they already were. Before she could speak again.

"Besides, I have a different matter to discuss with you if you would please follow me."

He turned and strolled down the corridor without waiting

to see if she would follow. He cursed himself at the feeling of relief he felt when she fell into place two steps behind him. *Of course she would follow. I own her.* As they rounded the last corner, he pushed open the twin glass doors to the garden. This was not a typical garden. Yes, it was filled with an abundance of all types of flowers, a romantic place worthy of a marriage proposal, but the river that cleaved it in two was mesmerizing. He watched her marvel at the birds of every hue perched in the trees. And he smiled at the terror on her face when a rainbow-colored bird landed on her shoulder, and he chuckled when several other birds followed. The rhythmic cadence of his heart swelled at the sound of her laughter. For a moment, he took in her curves and imagined how every day would be waking next to her. The way her warm body would feel pressed against his as she kissed him good morning before walking to the bathing chambers, taunting and teasing him to follow. Catching himself, he shook the thought from his mind and returned to the present. Moving in beside her, he cleared his throat and for some reason, he felt guilty, as if he had just taken something precious away from her.

"There is something I wish to show you."

He hoped this would make up for interrupting the moment she was having. They walked through the giant gazebo in the middle of the garden and followed the path to the left.

He cherished the twinkle in her eyes as she watched the stream leap off the edge of the garden. When they reached the end, Allister ran to the half wall lining the edge of the garden and gasped.

"Come, my dear, there's more."

He pushed back the potted plants revealing a hidden door. The winding stairwell spun for what seemed like hours before they reached the bottom. The darkness of the path was lit with the luminance of millions of glow worms lining the stalagmites. Ishtar's mind suddenly went blank when Allister turned and buried her face into his chest as a winged creature flew by. Breathing in her lavender scent, he shuddered as the hint of mint cleared his mind and was disappointed as she pulled away.

"Sorry, I was scared."

Protect her. I must protect her. The words echoed through his thoughts. "It's alright," he said, flashing her a smile.

She let out a shallow laugh and pointed. Her pearly white teeth reflected in the light of the glow worms, and in that moment, he made up his mind.

I will have her, he declared to himself as he offered his arm.

"By all means, we can't have you getting lost now."

She hesitated for a moment, before sliding her arm into his. He fought to maintain control of his body as the warmth of hers against his was slowly driving him to ecstasy. When they finally emerged from the mouth of the cave they were greeted with a view so breath-taking that he could not hide his smile when her jaw dropped.

"This is the true garden."

Allister's eyes scaled the waterfall and followed the stream back down to the large pool that formed at its base. Wonder and delight kidnapped her as she turned to see the edge where yet another waterfall began. This one, however, did not end until it reached the base of Ishtar's mountain and flowed out near the Den. Then his heart skipped as she looked at him. *Kiss her*, the voice inside him said. And while he fought to maintain the sliver of will he still possessed, her eyes drifted towards the pool.

"May I?" her eyes danced.

"By all means, please," he motioned for her to go.

Alli removed her clothes except for her underclothing and dived into the cove. Ishtar sat on a stone near the water and just watched. He sat in silence, not wanting to disturb this moment of tranquility she found. Before long, he went from watching to awkwardly readjusting the tightness in his trousers. When she exited the water, he had the strong desire to make

174

her his at that moment. He stared at every curve, wishing he could be any one of those droplets caressing her honeyed skin. When she dressed, she came over and sat next to him.

"Thank you."

"For what?" he asked, playing coy.

She turned to face him. "For this."

He stood abruptly to avoid letting his instincts take over. "Has everything been okay for you?"

Alli hesitated before she spoke. He understood why, but he was happy she told him of the mess of feelings she had about Ionis and how helpless she felt. She expressed that no matter how hard she tried, it felt like she was going to end up losing everything. He listened until she finished, then cast his glance toward the setting sun.

"Allister, no matter how you look at it, life is hard. You must never lose hope in yourself. When you do, that is when you truly will lose everything."

Butterflies attacked his stomach and he wanted nothing more than to place his lips on hers. Instead he shutdown his feelings and spoke. "Allister, there was another reason I brought you here. I have decided to make you a Lady of Valencia."

TWENTY-SEVEN

Resolve

Three days passed since Ishtar took Alli to the waterfall garden. Although she was overwhelmed by all she saw, it was still hard for her to sleep in the same chamber as him, especially since she had not replied to his announcement. She was, however, thankful that she did not have to share a bed with him. Ishtar offered to sleep in his sitting area until the servants could make rearrangements to his quarters. Breaking her thoughts away from the door separating her from the Routen, her heart returned to Ionis. She was determined to talk to her kindred today and quickly set about getting ready, but after their last conversation, she was not sure if she could. Instead, she found herself wandering the halls.

"I swear I have never met anyone as moody and mopey as you. All these mood swings of yours are driving everyone else around here mad." Erridus gave her one of her sarcastic looks, Alli gave an awkward smile before laughing.

"Can we go somewhere?"

"Where would you like to go?"

"I don't know." Just then, Narrock was escorted down the corridor wedged between several of Ishtar's guards. "Can we go there?" gesturing with her eyes.

Erridus grinned. "I suppose."

"Did you know your father wants to make me a lady?"

"I know."

"How?"

"I am the man's daughter after all," Erridus drawled, gesturing as if the answer was obvious. "So tell me, why haven't you accepted?"

Alli's eyes returned to Narrock as he rounded the corner. "This is not my home." Though, if she had to admit, her memory of her home was slowly fading. "And I'm not sure I want it to be."

"You know what your problem is?" Alli's entire body tensed at the tone. "You overthink things. Who cares?"

She did not know how to respond to her. Why did she care so much? The choice between slave and lady was simple enough. She could come and go as she pleased, and forget ever having to clean up behind these dirty males. In essence, she would be free.

"Is it really alright if I accept?"

Erridus clasped her forehead and let out an aggravated growl. "You do know my father is the Routen, don't you? For a dumb girl, you can really be stupid some times."

"I'm not stupid," she said, holding back her tears and trying to keep an even tone.

"Are you sure? If it helps any, your friend has asked for your freedom if he fights for my father."

"He did what?!" she shouted, stopping dead in her tracks. "Why would he do that? Nobody asked him to."

"Oh, gods help me. What is your problem?"

"Why does everyone feel the need to protect me?"

"Maybe it's because you are a weak, pathetic, pouting, whining, sniveling child." Alli's face cracked. "Does that answer the question?" She braced herself against the wall at the weight of her words. "For gods' sakes, did I not just tell you how moody and mopey you are? You make people—"

"Make people what?" pushing off the wall, she straightened her back.

"You make people see you as useless. Someone who *needs* to be protected."

Her words were like a well-placed punch to Alli's gut. Turning to run away, she suddenly found herself tossed up against the wall, pinned beneath Erridus' arms.

"Stop that. You are weak because you choose to be, and you are helpless because you let yourself be. If you want everyone to stop protecting you all the time, maybe you should show them you can protect yourself." She released her hold and took a step back,

As Alli was forced to listen, she began to understand she was helpless. Tears continued to form in her eyes, and then in a moment of clarity, everything focused. Flesh met hers as her ears rang violently, and the sting of pain exploded across her cheek. At that moment, she remembered what Master Centrine told her.

Someone is not truly helpless until they become hopeless. On the battlefield, you must never become helpless because if you do, you will

surely die.

She brought her fingers to the tender portion of her face and flinched at the lingering sensation. Then she swallowed her tears and brushed away those already descending.

"Seems she has finally awoken." Something between pride and approval danced on Erridus' face.

"I am not helpless."

"Then let's show them."

TWENTY-EIGHT

Loud-n-Clear

The smell of salt and blood brought back memories of the Coliseum as Narrock entered the large training space. Moving to the weaponry, he took notice of the quality of weapons to choose from. The weapons at the Coliseum were dull and rusted, and it was not unusual for them to disintegrate when wielded. But these were razor-sharp and pristine. It was evident just how much care each received, and these were just for practice. Being mostly aware of the conversation happening down the hall, he was pretty sure Alli was on her way here to prove a point.

Looking up from the weapons rack, the blood simmering beneath his skin boiled. Reynuck stood at the opposite end of the room pretending to train. he was not fully aware of why he felt this way, but every instinct he cautioned him to be wary of this male.

"You should have told them to leave the scar," Reynuck grinned.

Narrock resisted the urge to give him a few scars of his own. For the past three days of healing, he was aware of the invisible threads working through his body sewing his muscles back together. He marveled at the sensation of sinew and bone instantly reconstructed, and it irritated him that he was no closer to understanding this power than when he first experienced it back on his first day on this world. Ignoring his verbal jab, Narrock grabbed the gold-tipped spear and weighed it in his palm. These did not possess the quality of the heritage made on Jhatar, but he had to admit the feel was good enough. Holding it straight out, wanting to test his newly-restored shoulder, he took his stance and began.

With the spear nestled into his shoulder, his free arm glided across his body stopping at his chest. He bowed slightly before raising his spear. Held in one hand, he wrapped his fingers around the shaft and pulled the weapon across his body straight as the horizon. Eyes focused on the golden spade, he took a step forward into a crouch, slicing at the throat of an invisible enemy. Retreating in his grip, his foot launched upward, and the base of the shaft stuck toward the ground. Returning to position, he stepped forward and ripped the tip skyward. He shifted his weight to open his stance to the side. With his back foot, he kicked the base of the spear and centered himself on one leg. Rooted into the ground, he lunged into a bow stance and extending the weapon through another invisible enemy. He sliced the staff across his body before rotating to deflect a strike and downing another foe as the spear screamed from above his head before halting at eye level. Crouched deep, in a seated position, he exploded his thrust forward through multiple leaps and strikes. His movement was effortless as he deflected through his pivot and stabbed through the air as if he and the spear were one. He demanded, and the spear obeyed. As it snapped back to his side, he sent it rotating into a blur of motion shifting from one side to the next. His muscles moved on instinct as his mind drifted back to Jhatar. He attacked and defended, adjusting to every command from his father. As he practiced, his father grabbed his own spear and attacked. Feint, parry, thrust.

"Keep your guard. You're too tense. Focus."

He struck harder and moved faster to keep up with his father. And when his father stopped, he bowed before him. Sweat rained from his face—as he stood and he beheld the mighty Gwhin. The smile upon his father's face whispered of the pride he had in him. He allowed himself to release one tear that would be undetectable among the rivulets of water pooling across his body, before placing the spear back and letting the healers assess.

Among the guards who escorted Narrock, the Chief Healer was also present to observe his patient. He was keenly aware his breathing became labored thanks in part to broken ribs he received at Ishtar's hand. He tried hard not to show the residual effects. Even though they were healed, he could still feel where he required more. Turning to speak with the healer, his conversation was cut short as the Routen entered.

"How's the healing process?" Ishtar questioned.

"Apologies, your lordship. We only just arrived and have not been able to fully test his abilities."

"Well, please continue your testing."

Taking a spot on the wall to watch, Ishtar resigned himself to observe his fighter in action. Narrock continued where he left off. Pushing himself and willing his body to show no weakness, he increased the intensity of his training. He knew he was placing excessive stress upon his recently healed body, but he refused to let either of these males consider him weak. Besides, at this point, it was all nominal, and he knew his own body would complete whatever healing had yet to happen. He leaped through the air with grace and pierced with great ferocity until Alli entered into his area of perception. Eyes still closed, he dropped the spear and took up a standing squat position. With his fist clenched and ready at his side, he started. Every punch alternated—contracting and exploding. Opening his fist, he turned to the side, allowing his hands to glide through the air. Circling back, he returned to his original position and waited.

Alli entered the training room ready to stand up for herself when she saw Narrock training. When he dropped his spear and took a standing squat position, eyes still closed, she instantly recognized his request. When they trained on Jhatar, this was part of their regimen. Its purpose was to allow yourself to connect with your partner on a spiritual level. She hesitated for a moment, not sure if she wanted to accept, but then her gaze caught Ishtar and she knew. It was time to show them she was not useless.

She walked right up to Narrock, took up her stance, and closed her eyes. At this point, Reynuck gave up pretending he was training and focused all his attention on the two. When

Narrock did not move, She understood he surrendered the lead to her. So, she took it. The movements of this drill had no significance or order, and Alli knew that, but she wanted him to understand she was still a warrior. As her right fist exploded, he answered with his left. When she released her left, his right responded. She took a deep breath and stepped back three steps, and she began to shadow spar.

Narrock yielded the lead to Alli. After hearing part of her conversation, he realized not once since he had been reunited with her did he allow himself to listen. This time, he was determined to hear everything she had to say. As she led them, he focused himself to match her force, speed, and intensity. He felt her anguish. He was not sure what happened to cause this great exchange of emotions, but he sensed it. When he followed her into a sweep kick transitioning directly into a jumping spin kick, his eyes burst open and he was no longer able to maintain a connection.

Alli focused on making sure he heard her. She poured the emotion of her master dying, almost being raped, and the fight between her and Ionis into every moment. She wanted him to know it had not been an easy road for her over the past ten years. When she performed a sweep kick, she told him how she felt when he accused her of sleeping with Ishtar. She expressed that when she'd been so excited to see he was still alive and how his comment kicked her hope from underneath her. Her momentum threw tears across the room as she went into a jumping spin kick. She showed him her feelings of seeing him lying there dying as she blamed herself for not being strong enough. She sensed him break off, but she could not stop. Her warrior spirit was bleeding, and she had to tell him. She told him of her self-doubts and how her only wish was to be able to stand next to him as a warrior. Every ounce of her soul culminated in her fist as it jettisoned from her heart and connected with his face.

Alli's eyes flung open as her fist connected with the bridge of Narrock's nose. Everyone flinched at the sound of cracked bone. Unable to pull her fist back, despite the drops of blood, she realized he placed himself there on purpose. However, what caught her attention was the single tear that rolled down his cheek.

"I'm sorry." The depth of his words were etched on his face.

"As am I," she said barely audible.

They stood, and Narrock bowed slightly to signify the

exercise was complete. She nodded, and they both gazed into each other's eyes before he turned to pick up his spear and return it to the rack.

The silence was cut short when Reynuck spoke. "What in the Reinzour's kingdom was that?!"

"It is no wonder you, who refuse to allow others to see you, wouldn't be able to understand."

"You have no right to speak to me that way slave."

Alli watched flames erupt in Narrock's eyes matching the burning lava flowing in hers.

"Did anyone ever tell you how much of a pretentious prick you are. I'm willing to wager your fiery personality is because your bed is extra cold at night," Erridus said with a smile.

"Bitch."

Before he could regret his words Ishtar's blade was under his chin.

"I believe I have given you a warning once already. My generosity will not be extended a third time."

Reynuck raised both hands. Ishtar left him that way for several tense minutes before he sheathed his blade.

"Splendid," Erridus said. Reynuck turned in surprise to

see she was now standing behind him.

Bending over, she whispered in his ear. "Call me that again, and I will castrate myself."

When Ishtar and Erridus took their original places, Reynuck's anger got the best of him. "I am tired of this. I am the Reinzour's personal Shadow, and you will show me the respect I deserve."

"Very well, Joris, before departing this afternoon, I will be giving you a letter to deliver to the Reinzour. In it will be the detail of how his Shadow behaved while at my house. Of course, I will also make sure to compliment you in my letter." Joris bowed and shot a look at Reynuck telling him not to say another word.

"Wait." Alli's said, gaining Ishtar's attention. "I would like to give him a chance to redeem himself." She knew she was playing a dangerous game, but if he was serious about making her a lady now was the time to find out.

"Excuse me?" he said.

"I want to challenge him."

She came here to prove she was not some useless girl needing to be protected all the time and this is exactly what she was planning to do.

"Absolutely not. I will not allow you to fight him." Ishtar's face was stone.

"Father, are you suggesting she's weak because she is a girl?" Erridus challenged, lazily picking at her fingers with her knife.

"Erridus, this is not the time for your stupid games."

"Like I would fight a girl."

"Very well. Allister is useless, and Reynuck is afraid to fight because she is a girl."

"That is enough, Erridus."

"What? I just don't understand. She is challenging him," pointing to Reynuck. "Yet, you answered for him. And it is obvious he doesn't have the balls to fight her."

She was glad Erridus stepped in for her, but once again, someone had to protect her. "I am not weak or useless, and I want to fight him," Alli said pointing to Reynuck.

"Allister—" Ishtar said,

"No! Everyone is always protecting me and treating me like I'm inferior when I'm not." Her fists were tightly balled at her side as she stared down Ishtar.

Ishtar flexed his hands and ground his teeth. "Fine." Though it was clear he was not happy.

"I will not fight a girl," Reynuck protested.

"You will, or Joris will report you to the Reinzour," Ishtar said, eyes still trained on Alli.

"I will n—" Ishtar's cold stare choked the words from his throat. The murderous intent emanating from Ishtar's dark blue eyes told him he should not speak another word.

"She does not wield magic. Therefore, you will not use magic to harm her." He turned to Alli, "No weapons. And it stops when I say." She opened her mouth to speak. "This is not negotiable," he said with cold steel coating each word.

She closed her mouth, afraid of drawing any more of Ishtar's anger. Reynuck nodded his head in compliance before returning the sword in his hands to the weapon rack.

Both Alli and Reynuck made their way to the center of the room. Her eyes trained on him. Ishtar tried to lean casually on the wall, but it was clear to her he was far from casual. She glanced at Narrock, who took a crossed-leg seated position. *I am not useless*, she thought closing her eyes. She was thankful when Erridus stepped forward to call the fight before her nerves betrayed her.

"I don't believe in fighting women. So, I will let you get a free hit in. That way, you can see the difference in our strength and stop this farce of a contest." He dropped his hands to his side and waited.

Narrock snorted.

Alli wasted no time. She was quickly on Reynuck and delivered a bone-crushing blow to his nose. Instantly, blood gushed. Before he could even blink, she followed up with a jab to his throat forcing him to gasp for air. She connected a jumping knee to the same spot her fist landed earlier. He reeled backward, and she closed the distance with a giant lunge. She grabbed his collar and launched him over her shoulder straight to the ground. Unleashing two devastatingly quick punches, she connected with both of his eyes. Each fist's impact called forth swelling. He swung in pain, but she jumped back before he could land a blow. Blood oozed from his nose, and the swelling made it difficult to see. His bruised esophagus rived with each breath. When he stood, she was right there. She spun, and her elbow jarred his jaw so hard that several teeth were knocked loose. Planting her foot to terminate her spin, she redirected her weight and sent a destructive blow into his rib cage.

Narrock could no longer focus on his training. His eyes opened to the maximum viewing, and Ishtar's jaw was on the floor. They watched in amazement as she systematically laid into Reynuck, never once giving him a chance to recover. His refusal to take her seriously was his downfall. Meanwhile, Erridus stood there with a huge smile on her face. She watched Alli progress in the Den. Even though her father sanctioned it, she never reported to him her progress just to see his response in a moment like this.

Reynuck was furious. He could not think, and his senses were not processing information fast enough. Every attack he tried, she countered with ease. It was as if she could read his every move. He had not been accustomed to this style of fighting. As the Reinzour's assassin and spy, his job mostly consisted of catching his opponents off guard. Rarely did he have to engage in actual combat. Every missed attack frustrated him. Every blow she landed added coals to the rage he struggled to control. He knew the Routen was watching and he could not fight using his magic. All of a sudden, he found himself pressed up against the wall, his head playing a drum cadence as it bashed back and forth against the structure. Then, clarity sparked in him. *He said not to harm her with magic. He did not forbid the use of magic.*

As Alli gathered herself for another attack, Reynuck produced an aura of fire around himself. She jumped back.

"The rule is that I cannot harm you with magic," glancing straight at Ishtar. "You never said I couldn't use it." He took pleasure at Ishtar's face as Erridus burst into laughter. Reynuck released his aura and grinned. "Now, it's my turn."

With a clear mind, he hid his presence, and Alli was temporarily confused. As her eyes darted around the room, she saw Narrock, who returned to training his senses. She immediately understood and stretched her perception, but it was too late. Reynuck released his magic just as she closed her eyes. Her vision blurred and bells echoed in her ears. The next thing she knew, his fingers were around her neck, and he slammed her into the wall. She let out a scream, and he simply laughed. Responding quickly, she shoved her foot right into his groin. He crumpled to the ground, rolling in agony. Erridus was laughing so hard the only thing able to stop her was the momentary lapses where her guffaw got stuck in her throat. Alli stood to her feet and moved to attack, but he turned his aura on. She stopped.

Ishtar's patience was beginning to fade as Reynuck handicapped him with his own words. Forced to watch as she was helpless to attack, he moved to stop the fight when Narrock spoke.

"She won't forgive you if you stop this."

"I don't care."

"Father," Erridus said, all the laughter gone from her. "She wanted you to see that she does not require your protection."

Ishtar was speechless. He had not realized what she was doing until now. Returning his attention to the fight, he decided to honor her with the same respect he would give any of his Toultyn.

Alli could not find a way around his magic. If she attacked while his aura was active she would burn herself, and the time it took for her to expand her senses when he hid himself made her vulnerable to attack. *Think Alli*, she said to herself. Retreating to defense, she dodged most of his attacks. *That's one thing I'll give him*, she thought, *he wasn't wrong about the difference in strength.* Each attack that landed hurt worse than anything she had felt before. All of a sudden, Reynuck stopped.

"I grow tired of this. You cannot win, so can we please end this?"

Just then, she got an idea. *He can't hurt me with his magic.*

"What are you grinning about?" he sneered as he saw her smile.

"You're right. Let's end this." She charged him.

Reynuck rolled his eyes and threw up his aura, but when she did not stop, fear grasped his breath.

"Stop!" he shouted, but she pounced at him.

Reynuck panicked and dropped his aura, but in his haste, he did not think to protect himself. She placed every ounce of strength she had left into this attack. As her fist connected with his jaw, the force picked him up and slammed him into the wall. Erridus erupted into laughter again as tears ran down her face. Ishtar watched in amazement as Narrock touched his head touching the floor, a sign he has recognized her strength.

Embarrassed, Reynuck pulled himself from the wall and walked predatorially over to Alli. The pressure of his presence paralyzed her. He reached his fist back, lit it on fire, and thrust it forward with the intent to kill. She watched in horror. Ishtar and Narrock were both too late to respond. But, before Reynuck could attack, darkness took his vision. Erridus hit him with an uppercut so cataclysmic, he fell instantly unconscious.

"I hope you don't mind," she said to Alli, grinning ear to ear. "I just couldn't let you have all the fun."

The two stared at each other, sharing some unspoken bond no one else seemed to understand.

"Now, let's get you to the healing halls."

Alli stood and leaned against Erridus for support, and the two left the training halls without saying a word.

TWENTY-NINE

Respect

Ishtar stood in disbelief at what he just witnessed. Part of him could not help but gush at the prospect of a healthy Narrock, especially since he took on a Fire Lokai by himself. However, watching Allister systematically pick Reynuck apart was mesmerizing. As Erridus walked her to the healing halls, he found it incredibly challenging to leash his deep sense of longing to take her himself.

"There will be time for that later," he said to no one in particular. Turning his attention to a battered and bloody

Reynuck, Ishtar could not hide a blinding grin. "Well, I'm sure you held back, being the gentleman you are." Pleasure and exhilaration at what she had done to Reynuck filled his voice. "I am a man of my word. Joris, I have nothing to report to the Reinzour."

"Thank you, my lord. We are truly grateful." Joris grabbed Reynuck and forced him into a bow. "Now, if you'll excuse us, we will take our leave." Turning to his cohort and whispering only so he could hear, "before you saying anything else stupid." When they left, Ishtar glanced to where Narrock still sat with his eyes closed.

"Earlier. What was that?"

"That was the strength of a warrior."

"No, not that. That thing you and Allister did." There was hesitation, and Ishtar sighed impatiently. "I'm growing tired of all your dramatic pauses."

"It is called newaut. It is an exercise to train the senses. One takes the lead. The other follows."

"How do you synchronize?"

It had been a while since anything had captured his interest and he could tell Narrock picked up on this. He knew since he took ownership of him, not once did he show any interest in him. For Ishtar, it had been about his own objectives, and he had only seen the male as another tool, a pawn, in his strategy. Yet, after what he observed today, Erridus' words began to echo. So, he wanted to try to win the male over.

"We believe we are the greatest weapon. As such, we do not rely on that which does not come from within."

He did not quite understand, but he also realized Narrock did not trust him. "Very well. Allow me to start over."

He did not know why, but Narrock's unchanging face made him hesitate, and again his daughter's words nudged him forward.

"Welcome to my home. Within this house, you may consider yourself free. The only grounds that are off limits to you is my personal study and my chamber unless I've summoned you."

"I don't understand."

"I never gave you a proper greeting, and I thought it was owed to you."

Silence floated between them before Narrock looked to his wrist.

"Where do you chain me?"

He snorted. "I'm sorry, but I assure you, no one in this house will place chains on you. Unless you deserve them. You will have a room like all the rest of my men. Clothing will be provided, as well as meals and anything else you require."

"Then I require a room next to Allister."

"She rooms with me."

"What?! Why?"

He considered dismissing his question, but if his goal was for Narrock to fight for him, he knew he needed to earn his trust.

"There was a threat to her life. Those individuals are no longer living. And, to prevent any further issues, I moved her to my chambers." Before he could respond, Ishtar finished, "This issue is not for discussion. Let's be clear. I run this house, and should I choose, I will confiscate your freedom. It is not something I want to do. However, I will not tolerate being questioned. Understood?"

"Warriors of Jhatar protect our own," was all he said.

"As do I protect all within my house."

Ishtar surveyed the fighter's assessing eyes. While he was not blessed with the gift of wielding the elements, the strength of Narrock's will was greater than all of his Shadows. As he watched him uncross his legs and stand to his full height, he wondered for a moment what shaped him. Yes he knew the Coliseum was by no means pleasant, but it was nothing they had done that forged this monster.

"You will call me Narrock. Not boy or slave or anything other than my name."

"Very well." Standing at his full height in an attempt to exert his dominance as the head of the house. "And you may call me—"

"I will call you Ishtar."

Wind erupted from him shaking everything. "You will do no such thing."

As he stared back at the male, he wondered if these were the eyes Reynuck described as a pit of dancing fire when faced with the guard underground. The tension cracked and sparked between them.

"You will call me by my title as Lord or Routen."

"You are not my lord. and I will call you by your name as it is a sign of respect among my people."

His wind vanished. Surprise puzzled his face as he tried to understand the male standing before him. Erridus told him he fought to maintain his name in the Coliseum. Reynuck explained what happened with the guard. Then, he thought about his exchange with him in the healing halls. He was not defiant. He simply wanted to hold on to who he was before he was forced here.

"Very well. You may call me Ishtar."

THIRTY

Va'Luana

"STOP HER!" Routen Greyson shouted.

Va'Luana found herself in serious trouble. She came to the Reinzour's stronghold to make contact with an informant and deliver a message, and now she was running for her life. Greyson led a team of twenty Toultyn to capture her.

Val turned her head to get a reading of her pursuers. She barely dodged the flaming arrow that whizzed by her, missing by a finger's length. Stumbling, she gathered herself and forced strength into her legs. She could hear the thudding of boots racing over the rooftops as she darted down the narrow streets.

Out of nowhere, strong arms latched on to her. "I've got

her."

Without a second thought, she smashed the base of her palm through the man's nose. Before his blood could even start pouring, his body crumpled to the ground, lifeless. She knew she had to complete her mission at all costs. She took one look at the dead body and bolted.

The Reinzour's stronghold was atop of a volcano that lost its fire over a thousand years ago. When the Reinzour conquered this world, he built his stronghold directly in the middle of the ancient volcano whose opening now held a lake of water instead of molten lava. The Captain of the Voidwalker's militia informed Va'Luana the Oracle would be alone tonight. She was to infiltrate the Reinzour's stronghold and deliver a message. What she did not know was that the Reinzour requested Routen Greyson to keep watch over her while he was visiting Valencia-Commonwealth on urgent business. She managed to elude detection all the way to the Oracle's chambers, but when she entered her chamber, she was greeted by the tall, muscular frame of Greyson.

Val ducked and dodged the volley of attacks from the dragon-spawned and stonebreakers chasing her. Several times she felt her balance working against her, and she found herself wishing she had looked closer at how small the alleys were. Kinetic and element attacks whizzed by her as she narrowly dodged them. She could not afford to slow her pace to avoid the edges protruding from the walls. She winched every time she ran into one. Blocking out the pain she focused her mind on one thought, *If I can just make it to the water*. Considering she was being chased by a Routen, it seemed rather bleak. Just then, a wall of stone rose in front of her, cutting off her escape. She swore before survey her surroundings. There was nowhere else for her to go except up. The approaching sound of the Toultyn screamed that she needed to hurry. Eyeing a stack of crates, Val took off. She did not allow herself to consider if they would hold. Instead, she hurled herself into the air and hoisted herself onto the clay roof. No sooner than she did, did a flaming arrow pierced through her sleeve. Ignoring the burning embers, she sprinted for safety. Up ahead, Toultyn clamored onto the roofs. Her knees screamed with the sudden impact of jumping off the roof and her heart stop. She had just landed in a crowd of Toultyn.

She heard Routen Greyson's cry. She would not allow them to take her without a fight. She had managed to put a little distance between her and her initial pursuers, but not enough to take on this crowd and get away. Pulling out her weapons she glanced to her left and right and swore when she realized there was not much room to react. As she contemplated her escape, one of the Toultyn charged. He never saw it coming. Her spiked tri-blade claw hand moved like a hot blade through butter as it pierced both his eyes and skull. In the same motion, she flung her dagger behind her. His command to halt trapped in the gurgle of bubbling blood escaping his throat. Kicking the body of the soldier still attached to her claw into the incoming crowd, she reached into the pouch at her side. Taking out an orange crystal, the approach soldiers stopped. Val flashed a grin.

"Bye now."

The crystal exploded and a thick cloud of smoke enveloped the entire area just as Greyson appeared. A strong gust of wind cut through the smoke, but she had already vanished. After a few second Greyson arrived. Frantically, they searched the surrounding area.

"Find her!" Greyson ordered.

The Toultyn scattered. Just as they did, a horn sounded to the south. Val swore again. She was hoping to get away without a trace. The familiar sound of Toultyn, now flanked her on both sides as they gathered fire in each hand, set her nerves. As she prepared to dodge, she had just enough time to catch the glimpse of a third Toultyn's shadow from above. She slowed her sprint just in time for the spear made of wind to embed into the roof. This time, she smiled as she punched her claw through the back of his neck. The other Toultyn hurled fire hot enough to burn through armor, but she evaded with ease. His comrade, however, was not as quick. She rushed the attacker on the right pressing her clawed fist through his heart while throwing another vial from her pouch. Orange dust exploded when it made contact with his face. The smell of burning flesh filled the air as his screams silenced everything else in the area. To late. She was not paying attention to the environment and it cost her. She fell to her knees when a gust of wind caught the fumes of the acid and flung it right back at her. Fighting through the effects, she looked up and saw Greyson catching up. She willed strength into her body and forced herself to stand up. Staggering, she continued south. As she ran, she felt thousands of tiny blades slicing all along her nervous system as her strength faltered. Even though she knew she had the antidote, she could not risk getting captured. Dredge pooled inside her as she knew she could only use it if she could get away. She knew too many of her people's secrets and refused to aid in their destruction.

Stars crowded her vision as she felt Greyson's massive fist slam against the back of her skull. She clattered to the ground, her vision weaving in and out of focus. Suddenly, she felt her body lifted off the ground before Greyson flung her off the roof. Every bone in her body screamed as she crashed into the ground. Her body came to a stop only after it slammed into the half-wall separating the stronghold from the water's edge.

"Why are you here?" he asked.

Val forced herself to focus on the Routen. She hated his pale face, and as she took in his squared jaw and those blue eyes set against a field of white, she could not help but focus on the massive dent resting between his chin. When she did not speak, he walked over and lifted her by the hair. Without mercy, he sunk his fist deep within her rib cage. She screamed in pain. She was about to refill her lungs, before Greyson shoved her face into the lake. She thrashed and clawed at his hands. When they initially surrounded her, they had forgotten to remove her weapons. Her tri-blade claw sang across Greyson's wrist. He released her. Retreating a few steps, he demanded a dragon-spawn to cauterize the wound to prevent further blood loss. In that moment of chaos, she released the small vial she had lodge beneath her tongue and clamped down on it. The quick-acting antidote instantly cleared her body of the effects of the poisonous acid. Standing to her feet, she knew Greyson had broken at least two of her ribs. Taking a seated position on the wall, she started to laugh.

"What is so damn funny?"

Va'Luana looked at him, stood, and stopped laughing. "You should have killed me when you had the chance."

Before anyone could react, she lifted both of her hands in the air. A giant ape made of water shot out from the lake. As it breached the water, behind it, a massive wall of water erupted skyward. When she brought her hands down in a sweeping motion, the ape roared. Interlocking its fists, it aimed for Greyson and his men. Dragon spawned began heaving desperation attacks at the ape while stonebreakers frantically threw up barricades. As fire connected, it caused the ape to appear as if its fist were smoking. Their walls never stood a chance. Greyson just stood there. As the ape made contact, he flashed up a barrier of wind and fire, obliterating the ape's fist. He was not prepared for the tsunami that followed. It hit with so much force that everything within the area was decimated.

Va'Luana caught the current of the lake as it receded back to its place. As she plummeted toward the bottom she looked for the familiar opening. *There.* She found the small cave burrowed into the surface of the volcano. Pausing at the opening, she placed her hand on the surface of the cave, and as her hand swiped across the mouth of the cave, the entrance vanished.

THIRTY-ONE
Message Delivered

The edge of the stronghold was plunged into chaos. The tsunami destroyed buildings and killed several of the Toultyn and nearby onlookers. Those who survived scrambled to save as many civilians as they could.

Greyson stood at the edge of the water line. "How did they reach us?" His question was more of a demand than an inquiry. The stronghold was supposed to be impenetrable. Entry control points were established all through the incline of the volcano, and stonebreakers capable of altering the terrain against any adversary patrolled regularly.

Could there be a traitor? Greyson was lost in his thoughts. *It would make sense. How else did she manage to get into the stronghold unnoticed?*

He quickly dismissed this thought. These watchmen were the most loyal to the Reinzour and had the added insurance of being placed under powerful command magic. As he continued to think, he turned his anger on himself. How did he allow this to happen? The worst part was that he let her get away. He had not considered she possessed magic that could rival his. In his arrogance, he was too slow to react.

"Sir, the casualties have been accounted for. There were fifteen civilians and twelve Toultyn."

He dismissed the soldier without even turning around. Running his fingers through his hair, he clenched his fist before bringing them downward.

"YOU'RE DEAD!"

"Greyson, what do you want?" Rainiah asked.

Until now, she had been sitting in her chambers alone. The space was nothing special. Her bed was positioned against the south wall. She had a desk, and next to it was a full-length mirror. However, while the room itself was lackluster, the view was magnificent. From her window, Rainiah could watch the setting suns over the seemingly endless lake.

"Have you given any consideration to my proposal?"

"Are you seriously going to bring that up again?" she turned from the window to glare at him.

"Yes, I want you to wed me."

"As I have told you before, if I were to touch any man in that way I would lose my ability to be an Oracle."

"It doesn't matter to me. We can wed, and I don't have to touch you."

"So, I'm to be your *wife* while you run around getting your feel of other women, is that it?"

Executing a nonchalant gesture. "Well, at least now I can see you might actually care."

"Absolutely not. I care for you just as I care for the Reinzour's dinner parties."

"Don't you think that was a bit much."

"Speaking of the Reinzour, why is it that you decide to wait until he left to bring this foolishness to me?" She crossed her arms and tapped her foot. "Well?"

"Well, I wanted to get—"

Just then, the door to the room opened. They spun around to see a hooded figure. Before Greyson could speak, the figure reached into a pouch and pulled out a crystal. In an instant, dark gray smoke filled the room and corridor. Rainiah collided with the ground as Greyson forced her down and tried his best to cover her nose and mouth. Her heart drummed against her rib-cage. If this gas was toxic, she did not want to accidentally breath it in. However, despite all the chaos, Rainiah managed to see the intruder's face. As their eyes met, she sensed something familiar but could not quite place it.

Smoke filled the chamber, and Greyson darted after the figure, alerting the other Toultyn. When the smoke vanished, she ran to the window to watch as Greyson gave chase. Seeing the intruder was cornered, her hands drifted to her mouth as she watched the girl summoned a massive water ape and flooded the entire outer edge of the stronghold. She could not help the word that rolled off her tongue.

"Marvelous."

Remembering where she was, she quickly glanced around to make sure no one heard her. Moving to close her door, she noticed a puddle of water just on the other side of her threshold. She walked to her desk and grabbed a piece of linen to clean it up. When she placed the linen down, she realized there was a note hidden underneath the water. Quickly grabbing the parchment, she barred the door. Opening it, she read it and then immediately burnt it. As she paced, considering the contents of the letter, she half-jumped out her skin at the thunderous knocking at her door. When she opened it, Greyson stood there. Fury burned bright all around him.

"What the hell was that?"

"How am I supposed to know?"

"You're a damn Oracle! Isn't that kind of your job?!"

"Well maybe if *someone* wasn't in my room distracting me with idle talks of marriage, I might have seen it coming." Anger flared in his eyes, but she did not back down. "And besides, it doesn't work like that, and you know it. And why are you screaming at me when she probably came here to kill me? I saw what she did to your men."

He rocked his jaw at this realization. He was so caught up in capturing the intruder that he failed to consider this possibility.

"Sorry."

"It doesn't matter. The Reinzour is in great danger. I just had a vision. His trip to the Valencia-Commonwealth is a trap."

THIRTY-TWO

Sieged

Greyson ran down the stairs and through the corridor to where his Lokia was resting. Sensing her master, the Lokia lowered herself and he swiftly mounted.

"Guard the Oracle until I return."

As the Lokia thundered down the streets toward the edge of the stronghold, he could not shake the ominous feeling he had after hearing Rainiah's vision. As he charged down the bridge connecting the edge of the volcano to the stronghold, he braced himself as his Lokia leaped into the air and unfurled its wings. A gust of wind split the lake as its massive wings catapulted them skyward. Oblivious to the truth, the people cheered at the flying beast. He knew they understood that the flying Lokia had been reserved for the Routen and any other Shadow the Reinzour deemed worthy, and they assumed he was he was going after the intruder. But his heart pounded just as hard as the wing beats of his Lokia as one thought circulated through his being. *Will I make it in time?*

Travel to the most southern territory of -Commonwealth took seven days to journey. The Reinzour left nearly two days ago, and the attack would happen at the setting of tomorrow's sun. He had to hurry, and he felt terrible for pushing his Lokia so hard, but time was of the essence.

He covered nearly two days of travel in less than one. When he left the stronghold the sun was taking its place behind the mountains, giving way to the pale goddess of the night. The goddess was now standing at her highest point, and his Lokia was losing altitude quickly. Fear gripped the Routen, but he did not allow it to conquer him. Navigating to an open meadow, he said a silent prayer and prepared for impact. The Lokia hit the ground with such force that he was thrown from its back. Before his body hit the ground, he wrapped himself in a thick wall of wind. At impact, he and the Lokia cut through the earth leaving a deep gash across its surface.

Greyson awoke several hours later with a blistering headache. Gaining his bearings, he looked to his hands and saw they were covered in crusted blood mixed with dirt. Reaching to his temple, he winced. He knew he just narrowly avoided death. Shaking free from the distraction of his mind, he returned to the mission at hand. Judging by the location of the sun, he had nearly five hours to reach the Reinzour. Standing to his feet, he moved to check his Lokia, but she had already positioned herself next to him while he was unconscious.

"Thank you. I'm sorry to have to push you this hard, but we must protect the Reinzour." He cupped her face as she turned into his hand and snorted

She stared him in the face, stood, and offered her back to him. Without a second thought, he mounted, and they were off.

As he scanned the ground, he kept notice of the position of the sun. Rainiah said the attack would happen at dusk on the fourth day and the sun was already starting its descent. Just as his worry was about to strangle him, he caught a glimpse of the sun reflecting off the Reinzour's gold plated caravan that made no attempt to hide his location. Entering a rapid descent, he landed at the head of the procession. As the procession came to an abrupt stop, the Reinzour kicked the door of his coach off its hinges.

"Who dares stop me?" His question carried a promise of a swift death to any thieves delusional enough to attempt to steal from him.

Greyson was already kneeling, "My lord, the Oracle had a vision."

Looking to Greyson's Lokia, "Why have you brought your battle beast here?"

"The Oracle had a vision of an ambush on your caravan that was to happen around the setting of today's sun. Taking my Lokia was the only way I could make it here in time."

The Reinzour glared at Greyson. "Where *exactly* is the Oracle?"

He swallowed hard. "I have left her at the stronghold under the care of my Shadows."

"Did I not leave her under *your* protection?"

"My lord, she is safe, and my primary duty is to protect you." He raised his hand in a salute.

The Reinzour made him wait a beat, before ultimately returning his salute. "Tell me everything she said about this supposed attack."

But just as he was finishing his sentence, the caravan was under siege.

THIRTY-THREE

The Jeehiti

66 It's the Jeehiti of the Void," one of the Shadows yelled.

For the Valencian people, Jeehiti meant 'Of whom death is afraid; the immortal battle goddess.' And they were right. The Captain of the Voidwalkers had no equal in battle, outside the Chief, and she had been fighting this war since the beginning. She was fearless and the greatest obstacle to the Reinzour. She was clad with dark armor and sat upon an obsidian Lokia that dwarfed Greyson's. Around both, her rose-golden flesh and the Lokia, black flames danced. There was no mistaking the brilliance of her crimson eyes set against ivory hair and the shadows coating the tree-covered path. Her eyes met the Reinzour's. His nostrils flared, and he forced his fire to illuminate his golden armor. Greyson watched, momentarily unmoving at the silent battle for dominance—the Jeehiti of the Void spreading darkness and the Reinzour burning like the sun. He had been so distracted at the situation unfolding that he did not realize the Voidwalker who now had the drop on him. In truth, none of the Reinzour's men knew until a rivulet of blood rolled down their necks from where black blades were now firmly pressed.

"I did not come here to fight you." Surprisingly, her voice was serene and inviting.

In all their years of fighting, it was the first time the Reinzour could recall ever hearing her. He let out an incredulous laugh.

"You say you did not come to fight, yet, all of my men have blades to their throats."

"Perhaps it is for precaution. Or a sign of the incompetence of your men." Glancing from his men back to him, "Or maybe it is for your own protection."

His fire burned brighter and flared at the insult. "I will have every gods damned one of you killed and hang your severed heads in every town of this damn planet for your defiance."

"I believe the name your people have given me would tell you that I do not give a damn about your idle threats. Now, as I have said, I did not come here to fight."

"Then why the hell are you here?"

"I have come to offer you the chance to leave our home with your life. You and your people have violated the sanctity of our home for too long, and it is time for you to leave."

For a moment, the Reinzour was speechless. "Let me get this right. You want us to leave, is that correct?" She nodded. "Do you have any idea who the hell I am?"

"I'm quite aware of who you are Aditya. You are the sixth generation of the royal line of your family, and let's just say your lovers find you lacking in certain areas." At her last words, her lips curved upward.

"You bitch."

"Now, now—I believe we have evolved beyond juvenile name-calling, and if you haven't forgotten, your men are at my mercy, and you do not want to anger me. You may call me Caitlin."

Aditya took a moment to regather himself. "If you know so much about me, and I assure you there is nothing small about me, you would know I am going nowhere. This is my—"

"Do not say land because you colonizing demons showed up here out of nowhere and have stolen my people's land. So, I suggest you do not piss me off right now with your bullshit, and maybe you will walk away with your life. I have been fighting your kind since the beginning. And I will be here long after *you* are gone."

This statement caught Greyson's attention. *How could she be that old? She looks no older than her late twenties, early thirties*, he wondered, more to himself than anyone else.

"You will either leave my home of your own volition, or we will see to it that you are the last generation to sit on your pathetic throne."

Anger raged inside Aditya and his fire burned brilliant. "You dare challenge me!"

Caitlin smiled and let out a soft chuckle. "Oh no my lord," she said mockingly, "you, challenge me."

She flared her darkness and enveloped the entire area. In an attempt to answer, the Reinzour released his own fire to counteract her endless night. When he managed to break through her darkness his men had all been knocked out except Greyson.

"What the hell happened Commander?" the Reinzour snarled.

"My lord…" every word out of Greyson's mouth was shaky as his mind grasped desperately to reconnect to his senses. "She kissed me and said I had a pretty face."

Then, his body, unable to stabilize itself, fell to the ground, leaving the Reinzour the only one standing. As he surveyed the area, his eyes caught sight of the darkness that now covered his golden armor.

THIRTY-FOUR

Dinner Time

Narrock was still not accustomed to his new wardrobe. The fine linen, smooth velvet, and expensive cotton blends just did not feel right against his rugged flesh. In truth, had the servant girl not stolen the clothing he had brought with him from the Coliseum, he would still be wearing them. He stood staring at himself in the reflection glass. The white shirt, buttoned three-quarters of the way, fell over the black trousers with a single scarlet stripe down the side that hovered slightly above the white moccasins cradling his feet.

"My, my, what a tasty looking morsel you are."

Erridus was standing in the doorway. She lazily dropped her finger from her mouth and gently bit her bottom lip as she soaked all of him into her thoughts. He turned to look at her. "I'm sorry, it seems I was not thinking to myself."

He smiled at her. She stood there blushing trying to regain her composure.

"Don't worry, I am rather hungry myself." He turned back to the mirror. "By the way, what's for dinner?"

"Me."

"What? I didn't hear you," Narrock asked turning toward her.

"Pity, I guess you will never know," she said biting her lip. "But, to answer your question, we never know until the chef sets the table."

She crossed the room to where he stood and moved his hands out the way. Reaching for his shirt, her eyes caressed every inch of his chest. She mapped the path each of his scars took, committing them to memory as she finished buttoning his shirt.

"You are now a member of this house. You mustn't hold on to the unrefined ways of the Coliseum."

She picked up the neck dressing from the table. He bent slightly to allow her to place it over his head. As she did, she let her hands graze the nape of his neck. He shuddered in response to her touch. Pulling the dressing close, she tied it. Suddenly, she became aware of her heavy breathing. Catching herself, she realized his breathing matched hers. When she finished, she followed the dressing up to meet his gaze. Neither said a word.

Without understanding, his hands slowly began to run parallel to her waist, and he felt the desire to draw her firmly into him. He watched her eyes flutter at the nearness of his hands to her flesh and sensed her desperate plea for him not to tease her any longer. As he breathed her in, he was overwhelmed with the scent of honey and rosemary, that was until he was suddenly reminded of who she was. She was the daughter of the Routen. The savaged beast who killed his kindred after kidnapping and forcing them into this gods' forsaken world. And just like that, his hands returned to his sides.

"Not everyone can be conquered."

The weight of his words felt like a mountain upon her chest. She endured the pain, taking a deep breath.

"Well, then I guess we should be off to dinner." She quickly turned around and led the way to the dining hall.

Narrock was taken aback at the extravagance of the dining hall. This had been the first time he joined the house for dinner since arriving. He stood in the hallway unable to find words. The right side of the hall was filled with at least seventy-five Toultyn, and on the left, another twenty-five or so flanked the head table where Ishtar sat. To his right sat Alli and to his left Erridus, her eyes passing the silent command he was to sit next to her. He assumed the other men at the table were Ishtar's ranking members, and there, at the other end of the table was Reynuck.

Noticing his smirk, Ishtar asked, "What pleasure do we owe for the rare smile that graces your face?" His eye drifted to the end of the table. "Oh, so you have noticed the unwelcomed guest too?" Several members at the table held in a snicker. "For reasons beyond me, protocol dictates the Reinzour's men be seated at the head table."

"It is kind of funny," Erridus chimed in, "it seems he has finally found his place."

The entire table sparked into a fit of laughter except for Alli, Narrock, and of course, Reynuck.

"Very funny," Reynuck said, forcing the words through gritted teeth.

"What, that you are literally at the butt of the table?"

The return of Erridus' witty demeanor made Narrock wonder if the girl he had seen in his room moments ago was just another game she was playing. His thoughts were quelled when Ishtar stood and clanked his silverware against his glass.

"My fellow Toultyn, we are gathered tonight to celebrate the recovery of the House of Ishtar's representative." All in attendance erupted in cheers. "For those of you who do not know, this is Narrock," he gestured for him to stand. "As of today, you will address him as such. Any disrespect given to him will be considered an act of aggression against me." Every Toultyn stood and offered their salute. When he returned it, they took their seats. "In addition. You all know her as Hailey," the men cheered and whistled, as she was one of their favorite servant girls. "As of this day, you will refer to her as Lady Allister." The dining hall exploded into sheer pandemonium. Ishtar allowed the excitement to carry on before quieting the room. "Are there any objections?" Silence filled the hall before Erridus stood. "Yes?" he asked.

"Father. We of the House of Ishtar accept."

THIRTY-FIVE

Failure

The celebration went on for much of the night. Somewhere about halfway through, Narrock excused himself. The overdramatic show of frivolousness on his behalf was just too much for him to take. As he rounded the corner, he ran into Reynuck.

"Well, if it isn't the slave turned lord."

Narrock held his tongue. He observed and concluded that Reynuck just loved to be the center of attention. Without saying a word, He went to step around him.

"Where the hell do you think you're going?" wrapping his fingers around the upper part of his arm.

"Get your hand off me."

Reynuck chuckled before bursting into outright laughter. "That bitch has no idea what I could have done to her. And neither do you, slave."

Ripping his arm free, Narrock squared up against the male. On the surface, there was nothing special about him, but he knew what Reynuck was capable of.

"You're free to your own opinions."

"You're damn right I am. You know, I don't like you."

"The feeling is mutual."

He could not understand the aggressive behavior Reynuck was displaying, but the overpowering odor lacing his breath must have something to do with it. He shook his head in annoyance and attempted again to sidestep the male who deliberately stepped in his way.

"You, Ishtar, his daughter, and that bitch! I know they're up to something. He's plotting against the Reinzour. I know it! And when I prove it, I will enjoy watching his house burn to the ground. But not until I make that bitch scream my name," he said, spit spraying from his mouth as his body swayed.

With one arm, he slammed the drunk male against the wall and crushed an elbow into his throat. Murder tinted his eyes. Reynuck simply started laughing. Releasing his hold, the male fell to the floor in a fit of laughter. He turned and walked away, but before he could round the corner, Reynuck grabbed him again.

"Hey, you got something more important to do than talk to me?"

"Yes."

"What could be more important than talking to me?"

"I believe it's called taking a shit." He grinned at the look of disgust coating Reynuck's face. Then he left.

As he made his way back to his room, he came across the doors to the garden. Pushing them open, he strolled into the yard and breathed in the cool breeze as it swirled across his face. The air was filled with the scents of lavender and jasmine. Hints of honeysuckle and gardenia drifted subtly along the flowing river. As he followed the stream to the edge of the garden, he rested his forearms against the outer wall and allowed himself to be ensnared by the stars shining out against the silhouette of the night sky. He admired the brilliant light of the night sun and closed his eyes allowing his spirit to escape into the vastness of the night.

After several minutes he opened his eyes and noticed the stream did not stop at the end of the garden. He peered over the wall to see the stream poured into the deepness of the night. Kicking off his moccasins, he removed the neck dressing and descended the mountain. The climb was not as easy as he thought it would be. Many times, he found himself losing his grip as moss and algae attempted to throw him from the mountainside. When he finally reached the base of the waterfall, he was exhausted. Narrock removed his shirt and set it to the side to dry. As he did, he decided now was as good as any time to try to connect with Draxtin. He removed the remainder of his clothing and found a spot in the center of the cascading waterfall. Once situated, he steadied his breathing, slowed his body, closed his eyes, and reached for the Temple of Inderrah.

In an instant, Narrock was transported to Inderrah where Draxtin was sitting atop a small boulder.

"I was wondering when you'd return."

"It is not like you left me instructions. Anyway, something is wrong."

"What do you mean by wrong?"

"I can no longer harden."

"How long?"

"Since I left here."

Draxtin rested his chin between his thumb and index

finger. "I see. You haven't released your heart limits, have you?" Narrock shook his head. "Well then, you will not be able to use your releases until you have released your spiritual limit. Had you released your heart limits you would be able to use both simultaneously."

Narrock rose, his hands sliding across the top of his head. "Then help me release my limit."

"Of course. That's why I'm here." Standing from the boulder, he walked inside the gate towards the temple.

"Wait. The last time I tried to enter the temple I was thrown from the mountain back to my body. Why?"

Draxtin laughed from his soul. "My dear boy, I guess it means *you* are not ready."

"What! But you said it was important and the reason you came to me. Why bring me here if I cannot enter?"

"I spoke truth then, and I speak the truth now. What is it that you desire?" Draxtin walked over to him and placed a hand on his shoulder.

Images flooded his thoughts. He had never really taken the time to consider this question. Yet, now that he was asked, he found himself back on Jhatar sitting with his first master.

"Narrock, what makes us Gwhin?" his father asked.

A young Narrock answered. "It's because you're strong."

"My boy, we are strong because we *are* protectors."

These were the last words his father spoke to him before he died. He was five when he lost his father during a night raid by a neighboring village. He watched his father fight to protect him and his siblings from an elite soldier from the attacking tribe. The two fought with such ferocity that the only way it could end was with the death of both warriors. It was then that he decided he would be a protector.

"To protect."

"And yet you have failed time and time again. How can you call yourself a protector?"

There was no compassion in Draxtin's voice. Narrock thought about Master Centrine, the three Jazwon males who died upon arrival, Allister and the other two girls captured, every prisoner of the Coliseum that perished, and Asher. Everyone he tried to protect, or should have, murdered or enslaved, and his body swayed. The scars on his body burned. He pressed his eyes shut, but he could not unsee their faces. The sound that escaped his soul was devastating. Sorrow captured in hot tears seared his face on their way across his cheeks. Unable to support the weight of what he was seeing, he buckled to his knees under the agony of his failure. He bashed his head against the ground, an attempt to clear his mind, but in these spiritual plains, he found no solace from the pain. Then, without warning, the scar on his shoulder where Dro's blade pierced ignited in fire. He collapsed to the earth. Every scream a cry for relief.

"Make it stop…please!" he repeated over and over.

When his throat was hoarse and all the moisture from his eyes run dry, he lay on the ground wishing for death. He was not sure how much time passed, but when he finally attempted to stand, all the breath in him was stolen as he stared at the ephemeral souls of all the people he failed to protect.

Erridus knew she should have stayed longer, but she just did not feel like being bothered by Reynuck, her father, or any of the extra foolishness going on.

"Pardon me Father. I'm not feeling well."

"I will send a healer for you," he said.

"Please, that won't be necessary. I just need to get some rest, that's all."

She flashed her father a makeshift smile before kissing his forehead and bidding her adieus. Instead of heading to her chambers, she went to the garden and climbed to the roof. As she stared up at the starry night sky, Narrock's words from earlier echoed in her thoughts. *Not everyone can be conquered.*

She could not figure out if the pain she felt was from being rejected or because there was truth to his words. All the Reinzour's men ever did was take. They took this land, conquered other lands, appropriated cultures, beliefs, and stolen the uniqueness from every world they plundered in a desperate attempt to create their own history. They had no home. No place of origin, and yet, they owned so much of the cosmos.

Letting out a deep breath, she curled her legs into her chest and rested her chin on her knees.

Have I become like the rest of the men of the Reinzour's court?

A stray tear ran down the side of her face. As she wiped it away, her mind replayed the night when she watched Narrock stand on the edge of the ridge and cry. She remembered how he had not moved for hours.

"Was that the moment I decided I wanted him?" she said softly.

The night sky blew a gentle breeze across her face, causing the strands of her hair to stay suspended in the air for a moment before returning to her shoulder. As she gazed into the distance, a figure caught her attention. Standing at the garden's edge was Narrock.

"How did he get out here without me noticing?"

She watched him, in silence, when he started to climb down the side of the mountain. Her curiosity got the best of her. She quickly made her way to the secret entrance. When she reached the bottom, she shrouded herself in her wind and tried her best to remain undetected. As she approached the exit, she slowly peered out of the cave's opening to see what he was doing.

Did he fall? Panic rose in her heart when she did not see him.

However, when she saw his clothes on the rocks, she let out a sigh of relief before flushing red at the thought of a naked Narrock walking around. Scanning the pool, she watched for signs of him, and when she saw none, she gave up hiding and walked right out into the open to find him.

He was not in the pool or anywhere around. She glanced up the mountainside thinking he climbed back up. As she followed the waterfall's descent, she noticed a small split in the water. There, he sat in perfect stillness as his body cleaved the waterfall. She became so mesmerized that her words failed her. So she gathered his clothes in her arms and sat where they laid. His scent, a combination of woodsy smoke and sage, was intoxicating as she breathed in. Her eyes settled on him, and as she considered him, she found herself lost in him.

She was not even aware she had fallen asleep, but Narrock's pained cries jarred her into alertness. Jumping from where she was dozing, she stood with blades in each hand as she surveyed the area for intruders. Nothing. She looked to where he was, and she was horrified. All of his scars looked as if there were echoes of lava burning bright under the surface. When he screamed again, she leaped into the pool and swam vigorously to reach him. Before she could stop him, his body tipped forward and plunged into the cold water. She took a deep breath and dived straight down. Every stroke she took screamed her desperation to reach him as she watched the clouds of air pockets escape his mouth. Stretching her hand forward, she enveloped him in a dome of air. Without thinking, she flung him into the air.

Shooting streams of wind from her feet, she propelled herself out of the water. Her knees gave way as she landed and she let out a screech in response. Ignoring the pain, she raced over to him and examined his body. He was not moving. She placed her ear to his chest. Fear gripped her as she could hear a faint pulse, but she could not see his chest rise or fall.

Placing her palm on his forehead and grasping his chin with her hand, she tilted his head back. She pressed her lips to his and sent her prayers into his body, hoping it would be enough to return life to him. When the supply of air did not return him to life, she found herself beating on his chest.

"Please, don't die," her words breaking through deep sobs.

She breathed into his body once more and still no response. This time when her fist came down upon his chest, Narrock's eyes sprang open, and he became his own waterfall until he passed out.

THIRTY-SIX

Blurred Lines

Alli was hoping to speak with Narrock during dinner, but with everything going on, she could not find the time. When he had not returned, she grew worried but stayed until the evening was over.

"Good night, Lady Allister," one of the Toultyn said as he carried his drunken buddy back to his chamber.

It still did not feel right being referred to as a lady, but she was thankful for the protection it offered her. For much of the evening, she avoided being alone with Ishtar, knowing tonight she would be sharing the same quarters with him and he had grown tired of all her stunts to prevent it. No matter what she had to say, he would not let her move back to her own quarters.

"I will worry about that when I'm tired," she said and she quickly slipped out of the dining hall before the head of the house could spot her. Dashing down the corridor, she hid in a tiny alcove and waited. Calming herself, Alli extended her senses attempting to find Narrock.

"I guess I'm not close enough."

Extending the basic senses was fundamental to all the warriors on Jhatar, and while Alli could perform the task, her command was nowhere near Narrock's level. She continued like this all over the house while making sure to avoid Ishtar. She was finally able to lock onto his presence. She was not sure, but she felt as if he was in some sort of distress. Her concern for him made her sloppy, and she ran right into the Routen.

"Here you are. When one of my men told me you left. I was shocked you didn't think to mention it to me."

"I just needed some space. Your men can be a little too rowdy." She hoped she did not seem distant, but she was not ready for a prolonged conversation.

"You wouldn't have been off looking for Narrock now, would you?"

"It's just...it's his first real night in the house, and I

wanted to make sure he was adjusting."

Ishtar raised a brow. "You know, I never meant for him to get hurt. I should have been there to protect you in the first place. I'm sorry." He raised a hand to cup her cheek.

She was lost for words. While whatever *this* was, happening between them was undoubtedly alluring, she could not help but wonder if it was real. As she watched him, she could tell he had a little too much cider. This was usually when the Toultyn would become loose-lipped, making it the prime opportunity for her to gather information. She hesitated for a moment before she spoke.

"Why me? Why make me a lady?"

His hand glided from her face and gently caressed her shoulder and arm. "I have not known the touch of a woman in a long time." His gaze traced the path his hand made. "I was hoping to remove the barriers between us." Taking her hand in his, "I was hoping…"

She leaned in, desperate to hear the words flowing from his mouth. But, before he could finish his statement, he jerked his head to the side and released the entirety of his stomach.

"Allister, I'm sorry." Gathering what decency remained, he turned and briskly made his way down the corridor.

She stood there, mouth wide open until the taste of bile

coated her tongue, and she almost gagged. She felt that pull at her senses again. She quickly stepped outside to escape the putrid smell. As she crossed the garden, she paused to take in the night sky. It was beautiful, and after a moment of admiration, she continued to where she last felt him. Her heart stopped as she felt his presence spike and then stop. Running to the edge of the garden, she saw the covering to the entrance had already been removed. Racing down the stairs, she moved as fast as she dared. Several times, she almost lost her footing, but somehow she managed to stay upright. When she reached the bottom, she shot out of the opening of the cave and stopped dead in her tracks when she saw Erridus standing over Narrock.

THIRTY-SEVEN

Unforgiveable

Alli had not even noticed the heavens began crying. She did not feel the pitter-patter of the cold droplets land on her flesh. She was not fazed by the distant flashes of light. All of her attention was focused on Narrock's lifeless body curled over on his side. Erridus shifted towards her, breaking her gaze. The tears running down her face suddenly turned to rage.

"You did this," pointing a trembling finger at Erridus. "You did this!"

"Allister, it is not what you think."

"Say that when you don't have blades in your hands."

The rain started falling harder, and the lightning moved in closer. Erridus dropped her blades and stepped back.

"Allister, it's not what you think."

Erridus rarely made mistakes. However, when she unarmed herself, it was just the opening she needed. She advanced without a moment's hesitation. She rolled forward picking up the blades Erridus dropped. Even in her anger, she recognized the beauty of these weapons. The length of each blade reached almost to her elbows, and they were exceptionally light. She stood, holding each blade in reverse as she stared at Erridus.

"I trusted you," she said, her voice quaking at the betrayal.

"You still should," Erridus answered, producing another set of blades she strapped to her thighs.

She eyed the blades and noted that their length was nearly half the size of the ones she held.

"I should trust you?" A bolt of lightning struck the pool beside them. "When you are so prepared to bring death down on my kindred." She pointed the blade in her hand to the spot where Narrock lay.

"You're being juvenile right now, Allister. Would you get a hold of yourself! I don't want to hurt you."

"Like you did to him?!"

Erridus exhaled deeply. "Look, if you don't stop this idiotic act of proving yourself, I will not regret handing you your ass right here!"

There was an ominous shift in her demeanor. Gone was the calm, witty girl who made light of every situation. Standing across from Alli was the icy presence of one who embraced the darkness. A bolt of lightning struck right between the two, charring the ground, and when it receded, another roar of thunder filled the air.

The two were engaged in a deadly game of sword play. Alli was sloppy in her control of the blades, but Erridus moved with such grace and elegance that the darkness she commanded was beautiful. Alli arced both blades into the air and brought them slashing down towards her, but Erridus kicked her in the gut with such force that sent her flying backward several yards. Alli heard Master Centrine scold her as her hand opened against her will.

Never drop your weapon in battle.

"Stop this madness Allister," she demanded.

Screaming over the torrential downpour. Alli wobbled

like a newborn learning to walk. *Strange*, Erridus thought to herself, *why is her hair standing on edge?* Before she had time to comment, Alli darted forward. She swooped down to pick up one of the blades and lunged into the air. Swinging her entire body in a complete circle to gather as much force as she could, she brought her blade down upon Erridus. In answer, Erridus rotated her stance counter-clockwise and thrust her own blade upward into her attack. Suddenly, both felt extreme pressure bearing down upon their wrists. For a moment, they thought it was a result of their attacks, but then they realized their attacks had been stopped. Standing between them, gripping both their wrists was Narrock.

"Stand down," the threat in his voice terrifying.

Alli and Erridus dropped their weapons, faces registering shock. Upon impulse, Erridus threw her arms around his neck.

"I thought you died."

She could not tell if the water rolling down her face was rain or her own tears. She did not care. Her only concern was that he was alive. He placed one hand on her back and allowed her to stay there for a moment before he pulled away. He walked straight to Alli, rage burning in his eyes.

"Master Centrine taught you better."

She felt cracks spiderweb through her heart at the look

of disappointment in his eyes. Turning from her, he retrieved his clothes and scaled the mountainside vanishing into the darkness leaving the two women to talk. Alli looked to Erridus.

"Should we tell him about the stairs?"

Erridus looked at Allister and smiled.

"No, I'm enjoying the view a little too much right now."

THIRTY-EIGHT

Lorian

The large gold-laced doors swung open as Greyson entered the throne room.

"Ah, Greyson is here. Now we can begin," the Reinzour said.

Greyson looked around the throne room. In the center of the large room knelt the Commander and Deputy for Security, the Lieutenant of the stonebreakers, the Captain of the guard detail that accompanied the Reinzour on his trip along with the other six guards, and perhaps the most surprising of those gathered was Routen Lorian and his Second. Greyson, along with his Second, took their place next to Routen Lorian. When they took a knee, they all immediately stood at attention as was the custom of the military summoned to the Reinzour.

"Today, I want to honor the brave men and their heroic deeds during the recent attack to our home, as well as myself during my travel." His voice reverberated throughout the throne room.

Greyson watched as the Reinzour stood in front of the solid gold throne against the backdrop of the seal of the royal line, the Firebird set between twin swords. Beside him stood his mother—the sitting Queen as Aditya was still unwed—his sister, the oracle Rainiah, and next to her was Ronsoeul, he was something like a son to the Reinzour. The only ones missing were his brothers as they were in the midst of conquering their own worlds. As the Reinzour spoke, Greyson gazed around the room taking note of all in attendance. The front row was composed of what seemed all the slaves and servants of the house with those of nobility behind, and lastly on the outskirts of the room, the other twenty-two Routen and their Seconds.

"No doubt by now you have heard of the failed attempt on the Oracle's life, as well as the one against my own."

It seems no one had been aware of the attack made against him, Greyson taught to himself.

"While I was investigating the rumors of a traitor in our southern provinces, an assassin made a claim for the Oracles life." The Routen all looked at each other in shock.

So, they didn't know, Greyson thought to himself. The Reinzour raised his hand and the room fell silent.

"Thanks to the heroic actions of Routen Greyson, the assailant was unsuccessful. However, she escaped."

Greyson lowered his head. *Ah, this is to be a shaming session.*

The Reinzour continued, "Though the stronghold sustained great damage, the Oracle saw danger awaited me. Without regard for himself, Routen Greyson valiantly rushed ahead to protect me. Routen Greyson has proven his loyalty to the throne, and in return, I will pledge my loyalty to his house. As of right now, the House of Greyson will assume the rank of the Third House of Valencia."

The Reinzour led the hall in applause. Greyson bowed his head, before returning to an upright position. Erridus shot a glance towards Ishtar who remained steeled.

"Thank you, Your Eminence. It is an honor that I will uphold with my life." Greyson rendered a salute and fell back into place.

"Routen Ishtar, please do not see this as disrespect to your house."

"Of course not Your Eminence."

"Because of your military accomplishments and your achievements for the throne, the House of Ishtar will assume the rank of the Second House of Valencia." Again, cheers filled the hall until the Reinzour gestured for silence. "Routen Ishtar. As you know, it has been ten years since the Second House has been vacated after former Routen Dro attempted his failed coup. We lost many great men that day, to include my father." Aditya turned his head to the wall of Reinzours and executed a slight bow in the direction of the fifth Reinzour. "This appointment is of itself for a probationary period. Should you prove yourself worthy, we will hold a proper commencement ceremony at that time. However, should you, or any member of your house, engage in any treasonous actions against the throne, I will execute every member of your House and burn every person in your province."

"As it should be, my lord." Ishtar bowed deeply before rendering his salute.

"Now, let us turn our attention to the real reason we have gathered here today."

Greyson willed himself to remain composed. He managed

252

to improve his House's standing, and no longer had to depend on a marriage bond with Rainiah. However, even he found himself wondering, *what could be more important than naming the Second and Third Houses of Valencia?*

"But first, I would ask everyone to join me in the courtyard."

The only change from the throne room to the courtyard was that Greyson was ordered to stand with the rest of the Routen. As such, he took his place to the left of Ishtar.

"As I said inside, my travel to the south was to investigate rumors of traitors. Before I could reach my destination, I was ambushed by the Jeehiti of the Voids."

Greyson watched as the crowd whispered between one another and as some offered silent prayers at the mention of her name.

"It seems her desire was for me to give up my throne and leave this place. After Routen Greyson debriefed me on the activities that happened, I asked myself, how?"

As the Reinzour spoke, twelve Shadows walked behind each of the men standing in the center. The smell of burning accelerant filled the air as each man was outfitted with a noose and had their hands bound. Then, Ronsoeul erected twelve gallows behind the men using a form of stonebreaker magic called green magic. Fear washed over the attendees' faces. Even though the Routen continued to wear their masks of indifference, there was no mistaking that they were unnerved at the situation unfolding.

"Routen Lorian, you are guilty of treason and for plotting with the Jeehiti of the Void for my death. As of this moment, you have been relieved of your House and your life along with your Second."

Every Routen's face broke as they turned to Lorian.

"I have done no such thing," Lorian protested, meeting the Reinzour's stare.

"You dare call me a liar?"

"I dare challenge the truth of your accusation."

The Reinzour laughed, "Very well, then explain how the Oracle was almost killed, that the stronghold was attacked, that I was attacked while coming to visit your territory?"

"I cannot explain anything I had nothing to do with." his eyes remained true and unwavering with each word.

"Is that so?"

The Reinzour reached into his pocket and removed an envelope. As he read the letter, it was as if time stopped. When he finished, he had a Toultyn take the parchment to Lorian.

"Is not that your seal?"

He did not speak for several minutes. When he finally spoke, his words came out grave and weighty. "The seal is mine, but the words are not."

"Enough of this foolishness! You dare attempt for my life and then try to make a spectacle of me. I am the Reinzour. Don't any of you forget it."

As if on cue, every rope snapped tight and groan under the weight of each man as they were lifted to the apex of the gallows. The scene was ghastly—men gasped for air, kicking and twisting, trying to hold onto life. Then, with a flick of his wrist, the Reinzour sent twelve arching fire arrows that grazed the soaked ropes at their necks. Every noose burst into flames. As the fire burned more violently, every man's attempt to free themselves increased. One by one, the charred men stopped moving. The smell of burnt flesh and sulfur choked the air. The last man alive was Lorian.

"Even in death you defy me," the Reinzour said.

Of all the men hung, Lorian was the only one who refused to give the Reinzour the satisfaction of watching him flail around. Instead, he never took his eyes off the Reinzour.

"Very well. Since you insist on staying alive as long as you can." He turned to Ronsoeul. "As of today, Ronsoeul has been promoted to Routen and given the lands belonging to Lorian." He turned back to the burning Routen, "Let it be known the House of Lorian no longer stands. Today, the House of Ronsoeul is born."

THIRTY-NINE

The War Council

The War Room was different from all the other rooms in the stronghold. There were no windows, and the broadside of the room contained maps of every world they conquered. In the center of the room sat a long four-pronged iron-wood table with sides that angled outward. At the head of the table sat the Reinzour. Ishtar sat at the head of the left with Greyson sitting at the head of the right. The remaining Routen filling in the open seats.

"Will somebody explain to me how the hell Lorian was able to conspire against me without so much as a gods damned challenge?!" The Reinzour's eyes, resting just above his interlocked hands, scanned the room.

"Sir, how can we be certain that Lorian did this? I understand the timing does suggest he could have, but as I watched him burn, I'm not sure that I believe he betrayed you." Ishtar said.

"Are you suggesting my judgment is flawed?"

"By no means. However, as your Second, I have a hard time believing a Routen as a traitor."

The Reinzour studied him for a moment, "Very well. Let's entertain the thought. Is it possible I just executed an innocent man?" Gesturing his hand, he leaned back in his chair and waited for their responses.

Routen Vance tapped the table while he gathered his words. "Sir, you executed a man you believed was scheming against you, and I do not see the harm in that, if indeed he was. My territory is also in Valencia-Commonwealth, and I have worked closely with Lorian. I do not believe he would get in bed with those filthy Voidwalkers. This is wildly outside his character."

"I disagree," said Routen Grewal. "To me, Lorian always seemed as if he was hiding something." He locked eyes with Vance. "He did. After all, he admitted his seal was on the letter, did he not? And are our seals not carried on our person at all times? And did he ever report his seal was lost?" The rest of the Routen withdrew in their seats, unable to find a reasonable explanation for this last comment.

"You have made a sound counter Grewal, but that still doesn't explain a motive, nor does it justify intent," Ishtar said.

"Why are you advocating for him so strongly? It is interesting how *you*, of all people, are leading this charge when the former Second was responsible for the death of the fifth Reinzour."

Ishtar snorted. "You really are a prick," Ishtar said, head shaking.

"You're one to talk. Your Lordship, why is it your new Second, and the man that shares a border with that piece of *trash* Lorian, defending a man you deemed a traitor? I find it rather odd, don't you?"

Ishtar's wind howled for release, while Vance's stone-breaker magic splintered the table.

"Do not insult the integrity of my House Grewal," Ishtar said.

"He's right, you know." The growing tension stopped as everyone turned to Kahlani. "Motive. Why would he sell out the Reinzour?"

The room felt like a vacuum of nothing.

"I have a theory," Keylar said. "Lorian was ranked last among us. What if his motive was to spite the Reinzour? I mean, what better way to undermine his authority than to force this very conversation among his ruling court?" No one said anything as they considered his statement.

"Do you think he felt the ranking system was unjust?" she asked.

"It's possible. And here we are questioning the innocence of a man, which in turn leads us to doubt the sovereignty of the Reinzour. Subterfuge at its finest."

"And you two bastards fell right into it," Grewal said crossing his arms.

The Reinzour placed his hands on the table after several minutes of silence. "It seems we have come to an understanding."

After each Routen nodded agreement, the Reinzour's hand shot out in Ishtar's direction and slammed him against the wall. The invisible hand of wind clasped down around his throat trapping air from escaping.

"Let this be the last time you question me publicly under the guise of my Second." There was no mistaking that this would be the only warning he, or anyone of the Routen would receive. "The next time any one gets the idea to challenge my sovereignty I will make sure to erase every trace of your damn existence from this world." He released his grip and Ishtar crashed to the floor gasping for air. "Now, sit down and be a good boy, and shut the hell up. Do you understand?"

Ishtar picked himself up off the floor and returned to his seat without a word. The Reinzour's words choked the life out of the room and darkness filled every crevice. In the silence, he made sure they understood the cost of defiance, and they all sat a little straighter in the seats as they focused their attention on their ruler.

"Now that everyone understands their place, let us continue. Ronsoeul."

Ronsoeul stood and grabbed the rolled document in front of him as he moved to the wall of conquered worlds. Unfurling the material, he placed the map on the wall just southwest of Valencia and returned to his seat.

"We have received word of a particular exotic that resides on this world. It is said to have the ability to store energy and then release concentrated detonations at the user's demand. Simply put, after the tournament, I want it."

Ronsoeul picked up where the Reinzour ended. "This exotic can change warfare as we know."

The other Routen looked at one another, each wanting to speak. Yet, no one wanted to end up like Ishtar, or worse

Lorian. So they sat, unsure of the Reinzour's mood.

"How exactly will this change warfare?" Kahlani asked.

"There is a limit to how much of the elements you can wield at a time. What happens when you've exhausted your reserves?"

"I have never reached my limit—"

"You may not have, but what about the Toultyn in your command?"

"What is the cost to the user?" she asked.

"We do not know." Several Routen whispered among themselves at the statement. "Our scouts only provided us with the information that the technology exists."

The Reinzour raised his hand. "Even still, we have conquered worlds for less, and this will be no different. We are roughly three weeks away from the tournament. When that is over, we invade."

FORTY

Reynuck

This was just the opportunity to investigate Ishtar Reynuck was looking for. The Routen received a message from the Reinzour this morning requesting his immediate presence along with his Second. He figured he would have five days to complete his investigation since the trip itself takes at least two days one way. Something told him Ishtar must have been thinking the same thing, as a female Shadow now accompanied him everywhere he went. Although this complicated his plans, it did not stop him entirely from taking advantage of Ishtar and Erridus' absence.

Since coming to the House of Ishtar, he had been continuously under the watchful eye of Erridus. Every time he came close to the study, medical hall, or his private chambers, Erridus was right there. Her skill at sneaking surpassed his own for which he had been bred to be the best. At least, that is what he thought until he met this Shadow. For the past two days, he had been unsuccessful at evading her. Every time he felt he gave her the slip, she always showed up where ever he intended.

Figuring he'd lost another day, he decided to go to the training halls to blow off some steam. As he entered, he was surprised to see Narrock.

"I didn't expect to find you here."

Narrock did not even acknowledge the male. Instead, he continued practicing with the long staff.

"You don't like me, do you?"

Narrock paused for a noticeable second as he cut his eyes towards him before returning to his training.

At this sign of blatant disrespect, he stalked up to Narrock and plucked the staff out of the air. His face, painted with anger, was mere inches away from Narrock's, which remained plastered with indifference.

"You will know your place you damn piece of shit!"

Narrock rotated his head around his shoulders, each rotation releasing the tension building up, before returning his gaze to him. Gone was the face of indifference, as it was replaced with a smile and chuckle. Releasing the staff, he took a few steps backward and then moved to the other side of the hall. He leaped into the air, grabbed hold of the exposed wood beam, and commenced to raise his chin above the wood and lower his body repeatedly.

"Who the hell do you think you are?" he asked, walking over to where Narrock moved.

When Narrock fully lowered himself, Reynuck swung the staff. A loud crack sounded as the wood sang against his exposed torso. He released a slight grunt. For Narrock, using his hardening had become no different than breathing, but now that he could no longer harden, he knew he had to retrain his body even more intensely. Without giving it a second thought, he raised himself back up. This infuriated Reynuck. When he lowered himself, Reynuck struck his exposed ribs again with twice the force of the last. Thwack! Thwack! Thwack! Each time, Narrock forced the pain into submission until Reynuck hit him so hard the staff shattered and his grip faltered.

Narrock fell to his feet, elbow pressed firmly against his side. He silenced the hurt, and when he rose to his full height, teeth bared, he channeled every ounce of rage he felt and sent his fist flying straight through the wall.

"The hunter knows not to provoke the beast," he said,

turning his attention to Reynuck. "The problem for you is that this beast does not give a—"

"What is the meaning of this?" Allister demanded.

"Aw, Lady Allister, I was simply schooling this…beast on his place," he said, mockingly bowing towards her.

"You mean like I did to you?"

The sound that filled the air left the room aghast.

Narrock burst into a type of laughter that reverberated around the room. As she thought about it, she realized this was the first time she had ever honestly heard him laugh. His laughter was accompanied with tears he tried to hide behind his hands, but he could not contain himself.

Reynuck, burned with embarrassment from the perceived disrespect, flared his fire to his fist and threw a devastating blow towards Narrock. Though his punch was straight and true, Narrock swiped his arm in an arching motion, deflecting his punch while grabbing hold of his arm. Narrock yanked him forward and leveled a bone-shattering blow across the left side of his face.

When Reynuck's vision returned from black, he found himself alone in the training hall. As he brought his hand to his face, he was not prepared for the immense pain nor the massive lump he felt. He was not sure how long he had been unconscious, but by the level of swearing he was doing, he was grateful Ishtar was not around. As he gathered his bearings, a voice startled him.

"Don't fret, it has only been about five minutes or so." The Shadow assigned to him was sitting in the corner of the room. When he forced his gaze upon her, she replied. "I'm sorry, I figured you wanted to know." She rose without a sound and stepped outside.

Only one word filled the essence of his being at that the moment. Anger. This had been the third time since he arrived he had his ass served to him. As he stormed out of the training hall, the Shadow decided not to follow and left him to himself for a little while. As he rounded several corners, something crashed into his chest causing him to stop. When he looked down, he saw some random servant ran into him—or rather, he ran into her.

"Watch where the hell you're going, you damned slave."

"Do not talk to me like that," she said.

Before she realized who he was, Veronica slapped him, eliciting the same eruption of pain from when he touched his face earlier. Her eyes opened wide as she realized what she had just done. In one smooth motion, his hand was around her throat pinning her against the wall, her feet dangling.

"Every last one of you filthy mongrels will learn your place." His grip tightened across her throat.

"Lord Ishtar will see to your death if you harm that girl." He released her, and she landed to the ground awkwardly.

"Damnit! How do you keep sneaking up on me?"

He tried to hide his fear as he did not feel her presence until she spoke. He shook himself before reaching to grab the girl by the arm. Without wasting movement, he pinned her against the wall again.

"You will pay for your insolence at the place and time of my choosing, or I will be sure to let the House Head know of this." Throwing her to the side, he stormed off.

"Don't worry," the Shadow said, "I will be sure to plead your case with Lord Ishtar." Then, she turned and followed after him.

Five days passed and Reynuck knew his time had run out. Ishtar would be returning soon, and he had nothing to show for the opportunity he was granted.

"Good morning, you relentless hound," he said as he exited his room walking past the thorn in his side.

"You are too kind my lord," she replied, a grin of satisfaction rippling across her face.

In the dining hall, breakfast consisted of overly gritty grains, fresh fruit, eggs, and fatty strips of salt-cured boar. Reynuck dropped his plate on the table and flopped into his seat. Never had he failed a mission so poorly than he had these last few days. He sat there toying with his food while trying to figure out some way to salvage his missteps when Lady Allister and Narrock walked into the room. He watched as they sat amongst the commoners. Specifically, they sat next to, *is that the female from two days ago?* Then, as if the veil had been removed from his eyes, he saw the connection.

"Ishtar has three of them?" he asked to himself.

Slamming his fist on the table, the room went momentarily quiet as everyone paused and looked his direction. When they realized it was him, they quickly went back to what they were doing. Before he came to the House of Ishtar, he looked into the fighter Ishtar selected. There was nothing spectacular about him. They could not identify where he came from, and nothing appeared exotic about him. The only things of note were his insanely high tolerance of pain and that after his first year in the Coliseum, he had somehow not ever been defeated in combat. However, when he saw the three of them together, Reynuck remembered one more piece of information. Narrock's file stated he came to this planet with nine other children who appeared to be from the same unidentified region. Bringing his hand to his mouth, he leaned back in his chair.

"How is it that three of the children have ended up here?"

He knew four of those children died before the selection, *so why does Ishtar have three of the remaining six? Is he somehow privy to information no one has?* Rising from his chair, he left the dining hall with purpose. He knew his tag-along would follow, but he did not care. As he turned down the corridor leading to Ishtar's study, he heard the annoying voice of the insect who had been assigned as his babysitter.

"Lord Ishtar would not be happy to learn of you invading the privacy of his study."

"Then why don't you go tell him where I am?!"

He resolved himself to disregard caution. He told himself Ishtar could not kill him without first speaking to the Reinzour, which to a degree was true. Still, he knew he would have to uncover something about Ishtar to use as leverage. He forced open the doors to Ishtar's study and dropped a thick wall of fire behind him blocking the Shadow from following. He knew if he did not separate himself from her, he would not be able to find anything. As soon as he entered the study, he began searching everywhere. He pulled books from the shelves, rifled through drawers, checked for secret compartments. Trained for stealth, he abandoned every ounce of training he had received and destroyed Ishtar's study until he found what he was looking for. Underneath Ishtar's wardrobe was a discarded letter.

Dearest sister,

I am quickly losing my patience with my nephew. If he were not your son, I would have been snatched the very air from his lungs. It is hard for me to believe none of his father's qualities, or yours for that matter, are evident in him. If we do not do something soon, I fear he will reach a place where he cannot be saved.

Sincerely,
Alsteron,

"What the hell?" His eyes flared wide at the insinuation of the note. "There are no records of Ishtar having a sister."

He was not quite sure what he stumbled upon, but it definitely was enough to blackmail the Routen. As if right on cue, a large gust of wind displaced the wall of fire he created.

"I assume there is a good explanation for you, ransacking my personal study." Ishtar's control of his magic was unsteady as he slowly walked towards him, a cyclone swirling around him.

Peering at Ishtar, a slow curve bent at the edge of his lip.

"Tell me something, if you have no sister, how do you explain having a nephew?"

Ishtar's wind vanished as the anger in his face was replaced with confusion. "Nephew?" As he looked Reynuck over, his eyes landed upon the letter in his hand. "I am going to give you one chance to explain yourself."

"You're going to give me time?" he laughed. "I'm sorry. I don't think you understand the situation you're in."

"Boy, I am just about out of patience with you."

"Huh. I wonder what the Reinzour will say when he finds out you have been keeping secrets."

"Lord Second, you need not explain yourself to him," Erridus said.

"Lord Second?" Reynuck repeated with hesitation.

She looked right at him and smiled. "Let's see how well you fare explaining to the Reinzour how you destroyed the Second's study, openly defied him in his House, and tarnished the name of the Reinzour by being an overall," she paused to consider the right choice of words, "ah, dick."

The genuine fear that unveiled across his face was met with her playful smile.

Reynuck felt so stupid. If only he looked at the letter more carefully, he would have seen the name at the bottom of the paper. Storming through the corridors, his pride demanded he enforce his dominance today to make up for all the contemptuous losses he experienced. Then, as if fate was smiling upon him, Veronica appeared before him. He stalked over to her, and those near her quickly vacated.

"You will come to my chambers and you will tell *no one.* Or, you will forfeit your life. Do you understand?" he whispered so only she could hear.

She nodded in understanding.

"Good, do not make me wait long."

While he waited for Veronica, his hatred of both the Routen and Second grew.

"Who the hell do they think they are?" he murmured to himself. His question was met with the mocking reply he heard earlier. *Why did the Reinzour make that bastard the Second? I was supposed to have taken that position.* Just then, there was a soft knock at the door. "Enter," he said, not bothering to open the door himself.

"You wanted to see me?" Veronica asked, entering the room.

"Ah, yes. Close the door."

As she closed the door behind her, he moved from his position by the window to sit in the chair next to the desk.

"Do you understand the error of your actions earlier?"

"Sir, my sincerest apologies. I was careless."

Reynuck looked the young servant up and down. Her flesh was like the flesh of a ripened peach that hung from the vines of her short-cut hair. As his eyes continued to peruse from her small chest down to her curved waist and back up, his need to prove his dominance was heightened.

"There are two others in this house that look like you. Who are they to you?"

"They are my kindred."

He was baffled. As he looked at her, it almost seemed like she harbored malice against them. "Why do they have positions of importance in this house, and you don't?"

"I don't know."

"No matter. I'm sure your kindred have been advocating for you to no longer be a slave."

This time, it was he who looked away. He allowed his sight to drift to the window, all the while keeping a studying eye on her.

"They have done their best to ensure I am taken care of."

Her response was choked, and he knew what he saw earlier was indeed true. This girl harbored negative feelings towards her kindred.

"But you're still a slave, yet they walk around free?"

Desperate to change the direction of the conversation, she said, "My Lord, I am sure you didn't call me to your chamber to discuss—"

Instantly, he pinned her against the wall, his hand finding the familiar placement around her throat.

"I am the Reinzour's Shadow. I will not be handled as anything less. Not by him, that bitch, nor those damn dressed up slaves, and definitely," he paused, drinking in the fear displayed in her eyes, "not you." Then, he leaned forward and pressed his lips against hers.

She bit down on his lip, drawing blood, before pushing him off. In answer, he slapped her so hard she fell to the ground.

He grabbed her by the hair and again pinned her to the wall. That same tendril of fear spread throughout her body. Again, he pressed his lips against hers, and on cue, she pushed him away. Yet, this time she did not bite him. Gone was the fear and instead there was nothing. Reynuck wrapped his hand around her neck again. She let out a soft cry.

"What game are you playing, girl?" She said nothing.

275

"Answer me," he said as he struck the backside of his hand against her face.

Ionis could not understand why she was the only one of her kindred in this situation. The cries she had been releasing in response to his man-handling faded. Her entire body began to slack, and all she could think about was being somewhere else.

Reynuck grabbed a hand full of hair and yanked her sideways. She bit her lip to stifle her scream. No one was coming for her and she knew that. No one ever came when it came to her. There was an explosion of pain at the back of her skull and stars dotted her vision as Reynuck slammed her against the wall. She did not even bother trying to clear the stars. Instead, she dove deeper within herself, hoping to find a place to disappear. With a jolt, she snapped back to reality, salt staining her face as he slapped her across her face, harder than before. She desired nothing more at that moment then to just stop existing. She was pulled from the unforgiving surface of the wall and thrown on the bed where Reynuck kissed her deeply. She struggled to push him away, but this time, when her eyes glazed over, he knew he won. He pulled away and studied her face. There was no doubt about it. This victory was his. With the need to satisfy his ego, he took it.

He grabbed her neck as he peppered rough kisses

down her body. He pulled up her shirt, ripped through her undergarments, and latched onto her small breast. He massaged them gently until he punished them for producing no milk. Her head fell to the side. He moved downward in search of anything to quench his thirst. Discarding her skirt and undergarment, he forced her legs apart. He refused to look at her. He was of statue and she was nothing. *Good*, he thought, his ego shouting in triumph. Then he went searching. He traveled the track from her inner thigh up towards the swell of the sweet scent of promise. When he reached the well, he found himself examining the taste. With each flick and graze, Ionis' grip on reality began to give way. Reynuck immersed himself and began to drink with fervor. Her head buried in the bed, hands grabbing on for dear life, her cries of stop ignored. And when he drunk his fill, he flipped her over and dominated her until she was left there in silence.

FORTY-ONE

Apology

The next morning, Ishtar set out to handle Reynuck after putting his study back together.

"You need to be more careful, I don't need to explain to you what is at stake, do I?" Her voice had none of the witty banter she was known for. Instead, it was hard and almost scolding.

Letting out a sigh. "I know. I didn't expect him to destroy my office in search of the secrets of our house."

For several minutes, their conversation continued discussing the nature of the spy residing in their house. As if the demon heard his name, there was a knocking at the door.

Reynuck entered the room and knelt before him.

"I would like to apologize for my rude behavior since my arrival. I allowed my pride and ego to swell and considered my position to be greater than yours. I now understand I was a fool."

Ishtar and Erridus were taken aback. The worst part was that neither of them could detect any malice or dishonesty in his apology. He appeared to be genuinely remorseful.

"Please understand, I don't expect your immediate forgiveness, and I wouldn't blame you if you completely dismissed me right now. However, I would like the opportunity to prove myself and not defile the name of the Reinzour, as I was sent here on his behalf." He bowed even further before lifting his gaze to meet Ishtar's.

Ishtar said nothing. Clearly, the same puzzlement he felt also reflected in his daughter, who made no effort to hide the confusion on her face. He was left with two choices: continue in the path he decided earlier, or change the plan. Erridus spoke.

"Look, father, he grovels. Tell me something, how much of your weak a—" she caught herself, remembering she was still in her father's presence, "excuse is because father is now the Second?" Ishtar did not say it, but he was grateful for the inquiry.

Reynuck considered her words. "Routen Ishtar's promotion has no bearings on my actions." His attention shifted from Erridus to Ishtar. "After yesterday's accusations, I came to realize I dishonored myself by forcibly trying to expose a picture that was self-imposed."

Not missing a beat, she honed in on what he had just said. "What do you mean by *a picture that you self-imposed*? Have you been trying to shame my father's House?!"

Dropping his head, Reynuck answered. "I will not apologize for doing my job. I am the Reinzour's spy and have a responsibility to protect his interests. As the stories are told, Routen Dro attempted to overthrow the Reinzour, and as such, the position of Second had been vacant for a decade. I had to ensure that you carried no treasonous nature before the Reinzour."

Ishtar held a neutral disposition, but considered his words carefully—*had I been considered for the position of Second before his visit?* The revelation of this question certainly would explain the male's behavior since his arrival.

"You have transgressed against me, and here you seek salvation. You have no honor, and I am not inclined to heed your apology."

"I understand. Then please allow me the opportunity to

make amends."

Erridus spoke. "You know Father, he had such an aversion for our servants." Then, the devil smiled.

"It seems my daughter feels you could stand to learn humility."

"If it will allow me the chance to return to a favorable standing in your sight, very well."

Reynuck forced himself to hide his contempt at the direction this was going. In all his years, there was never a distinction between slave and servant, and now, he was being faced with the ultimate slap to the face.

"Then it is settled. You will share in the servant duties for the remainder of your stay." Turning to Erridus. "Please ensure the staff is made aware, and I expect all reporting on our new servant to be directed straight to you."

"Yes, Father." She looked to Reynuck, "I believe the stalls have yet to be mucked. I will have him start there."

"Now, be gone," he turned and went back to studying an open book at his desk.

Reynuck stood and bowed before exiting the room.

"I don't trust him," Erridus said. Her father nodded in agreement.

On the other side of the door Reynuck's body trembled as he fought to keep his anger in check. The most significant error he made yesterday was not paying attention to the name on the bottom of the letter. As a result, he knew he was in danger of the wrath of Ishtar. He meant to stifle the Routen's ire by coming to apologize, but he had not planned on Erridus being with him. Her suggestion that he become a slave was infuriating, and the fact Ishtar agreed was maddening. He clenched his teeth as he walked down the corridor. Still, he was confident that while they did not trust him, they no longer suspected him of continuing his attempt to destroy this house. He reminded himself of his training. A spy must become like the chameleon, and he was now determined to prove why the Reinzour had personally chosen him.

FORTY-TWO

Lessons from the Wise

When it came to training, everything had always been easy for Narrock. Back on Jhatar, he was considered a prodigy. Of course, it helped his father was one of the elite Gwhin—even among the Gwhin his father was deemed to be legendary. Since he was old enough to walk, his father drilled him in the ways of the warrior, but even with a life dedicated to training, this was one lesson he continued to fail.

"In life, failure is our greatest teacher." Draxtin said, sitting crossed-legged atop the boulder.

"I don't care! The tournament is in two weeks, and I still cannot harden."

Rising from his seat, Draxtin walked to the younger warrior, fist clenched. "Ready yourself."

He settled in his stance, trepidation climbing up his spine. He could tell his ancestor was angry. He opened his mouth to offer amends, but before he could part his lips, Draxtin was on him. They fought without weapons, and he was forced to bear the brunt of his ancestor's might. Even though they existed in an ephemeral state, he felt the weight of every blow.

"You are a disgrace to every warrior of Jhatar," he shouted as he landed several blows.

The first blow caught him in the throat, causing him to immediately collapse to the ground; however, before his body had fallen, Draxtin unleashed a devastating upward thrust launching him into the air. Leaping into the air, the mighty Gwhin rocketed Narrock's body into the ground with a vengeful ax kick. Narrock thought he was going to indeed die as every ounce of breath was cleaved from his body. As he sucked in as much air as his lungs would allow, he found himself rolling around on the training ground desperate to return his breath to normal. Draxtin dusted himself off before returning to his seat.

"If failure is a warrior's greatest teacher, what valuable lesson did you just learn?"

Pushing himself up from the ground and resting on all fours, Narrock conceded.

"I'm sorry."

"Save it! For three weeks, you have continued to ignore your teacher. Instead, you allow your pride to continue to lead you toward destruction."

"I am a warrior. It is my pride that keeps me—"

"It is your pride that holds you back. Or have you forgotten? You don't care about those you claim you want to protect. Your only concern is that they never see you as weak. Pathetic."

"You're wrong," he said, shaking his head.

"Am I? Then explain yourself," the older warrior challenged.

With a swipe of his hand, instantly they left Inderrah. He found himself back at the night after he left the Coliseum with Ishtar. He remembered staring at the sky and crying for the first time. He mourned those he lost but in his heart expressed gratitude to have known at least Allister survived among his kind. Then he watched in shame as he heard the conversation he had with her that night.

285

"Tell me, how do you feel after opening your legs to the people who killed our family?"

He was repulsed by his words.

"Tell me, young warrior, where was the concern for protection when you spoke these words?"

"I, I didn't mean to hurt her."

"Of course you didn't. Your only thought was to shame her by exalting yourself as nothing more than a righteous prick."

"No, I—"

"You what? All hail the mighty Narrock as he fights for his life while the whore Allister forgot where she came from."

"That's not it!"

"Then what is it? Why else would you speak such shameful words?!"

"I didn't mean—"

"Of course you didn't." Again, there was no sympathy in his words. "Did you ever stop to think about what life had been like for her during these last ten years? Certainly not. And why would you, you narcissistic glory whore."

"You're wrong."

He tried, but failed to keep his tears at bay. He knew the truth of his ancestor's words even as he tried to defend himself.

He knew why he said what he had. He wanted her to know he stayed true despite the hardship. He insulted her warrior spirit because he desired to shame her. The dams could no longer hold back his tears.

"You will not have my pity, you arrogant child. The prideful warrior is the one who only receives the glory of his precious ego. You," he pointed to him, "have your glory."

The ground turned to mud under the sobbing male. The realization of his failure as a warrior broke him. He told himself everything he had done since the beginning was for the sake of protecting others, but as he pulled back the lie, he saw it was to exalt himself. No one must have told Draxtin about not kicking a person when they were down because, despite Narrock's visible brokenness, he continued to berate him. Every rebuke cut deep, and every admonishment crushed him until he had nothing left, until he was nothing.

"I don't deserve to be a warrior."

Hearing his own words, and the conviction in them, quenched the remaining embers of his spirit. Curling in on himself, Narrock nestled his head between his arms and pressed himself against the ground. Draxtin paused. Then he allowed a smile to don his face.

"I believe today, you have learned a valuable lesson,

young warrior." As the older warrior knelt beside him, he placed

his hand upon Narrock's shoulder. "The warrior who seeks his

own glory is incapable of protecting anything else."

FORTY-THREE

The Warrior's Spirit

66 What is wrong with your friend?" Erridus asked when Alli arrived to the training halls.

Ever since his last journey to Inderrah, Narrock had been different. Many who could not match the male in sparring easily bested the fighter, and Ishtar's anger did not help the situation.

"You're supposed to represent my House in less than

two weeks, and this is the best you can offer!"

Alli watched as Narrock lowered his head and said nothing. Any other time, he would have asserted himself and challenged Ishtar, but to see him become so meek and docile was sickening for her to watch. Then as if he sensed dying prey, Reynuck arrived.

He had been on his best behavior lately, making sure not to expose his deep-seated hatred of his slave duties. Though he had not learned anything since Ishtar's return, he did manage to find he was not the only person concerned by the behavior of the Routen. It seems several of Ishtar's house mates secretly despised the new lady of the house. It had been a fortunate benefit of his slave duties as he was suddenly exposed to the sincere hearts of the people of House Ishtar. The head slaves were appalled. This girl was offered status, yet, they were never considered. Several of his head guards could not understand the freedom provided to Narrock and Allister when it had never been done in the past. And then there was the matter of sharing the same quarters which even Reynuck found downright disgraceful. None-the-less, when Reynuck entered the hall, he did his best to retain his humble demeanor.

"Routen, maybe he feels no challenge from your men. Maybe I could provide him one."

Alli listened in disgust, but the pathetic showing Narrock displayed was even more revolting. At least she knew he would not allow Reynuck to best him. Ishtar gave Reynuck a sideways glance before gesturing with his hand his approval. Reynuck hid a grin. Finally, he would be able to return the insult of defeat, allbeit to an already defeated Narrock.

"Routen, maybe it would also help if I were not to be hampered by restrictions? It is a strategy employed by the masters of the Reinzour to help trainees break through their ceilings."

He peered up through a lowered bow. Reluctantly, Ishtar agreed. Alli could not believe what she heard. How could he allow him to use his elements when Narrock was incapable of using them himself? There had to be something she was missing.

"Begin," Ishtar said.

Without hesitation, Reynuck was upon Narrock, fist blazing like a furnace. Narrock easily avoided his attacks, but there was still no life to his movements.

"Interesting. Has Reynuck gotten faster?" Erridus said.

"No," she said.

She had sparred with both males and knew the truth. Narrock simply was not trying. That is when it happened. Reynuck connected. Anger burned in her as the force from his

291

blow launched Narrock face first into the wall. From where she stood, she saw the triumph wash across Reynuck's face as, in an instant, he was within Narrock's guard. He unleashed an arsenal of volleys to his body, face, kicks to the lower body, and while many were blocked, several connected. Soon the room was filled with the smell of charred flesh.

Alli found herself in a daze. She had not realized her body moving forward, her hair standing on its ends, nor did she remember tossing Erridus away as she tried to hold her back. Even the look of fear that gripped Ishtar's face was absent to her. The only thing she could see was the fight before her. It was as if time stood still as Reynuck jumped back and propelled himself forward. His right hand burning brighter and more intense as the distance closed. Narrock, his back pressed against the wall, was barely able to maintain his guard. She found herself standing between the fighters as Reynuck's attack was about to land. She faced the defeated warrior, raised her hand, and with all the might she possessed, she smacked Narrock across his face.

"When did you lose your warrior's spirit?"

Charged aggression lit her face as his head snapped back into place. Her eyes softened as he stared back at her, tears running down his face.

"Alli, I'm sorry. For what I've said, what I've done. I'm not worthy of being a warrior."

She flashed back to the last time she saw him cry. Then she remembered. Cupping his face, a tear caressing her cheek.

"We are warriors of Jhatar," she said.

He looked away. "No, I am a failure. No warrior would have ever spoken to you like I did."

Remembering a lesson she learned from Master Centrine when she could not master the fundamentals of her training, she spoke to him in their native tongue.

"Warriors must face the challenges before them with humility and forgiveness," she forced his eyes to meet hers, "these are the battles that prove our worth as warriors. We must stay humble to the process and forgive ourselves all while acknowledging our weaknesses. Only then can we forgive others in their weakness." She took him by both his hands and pulled him from the wall. "You are my brother and have no need to ask for forgiveness." With nothing left to say, she embraced him.

A few minutes passed before the silence was broken as Ishtar cleared his throat. She pushed herself back unsure of how she ended up embracing Narrock. When she turned to Ishtar, face reddened, she could not help but notice an unconscious Reynuck slumped across the room.

"Care to explain how you did that?" Ishtar asked.

"Did what?" she looked at him, a blank stare plastered on her face.

"Knocked Reynuck on his ass," Erridus said as she laughed herself to tears.

"Erridus!" Ishtar cried.

"What? I'm sorry I couldn't help it."

Alli stood there bewildered. She honestly had no answer to what had happened as it was explained to her. She found herself apologizing to Erridus for what she had done. However, in the back of her mind she was baffled by what she was told.

There is no way I could have done that, she thought to herself.

Yet, she could not begin to understand what happened next. As she listened, she could not believe she deflected Reynuck's attack. Even more unbelievable was that the force of his attack seemed to double as it was returned back to him.

How? I am no one special to be favored by the celestials. She could not understand or begin to offer any kind of explanation. She was only returned to reality when she felt someone take her hand in theirs.

"Thank you," Narrock said before collapsing to the ground.

There was a quick scramble to get him to the healing halls, but if no one else saw it, she did. The spirit of the warrior was reborn.

FORTY-FOUR

Time Begins Again

Val was the last to enter the special council meeting. Caitlin convened this meeting after the report she received. Val planned to be early for the meeting, but the argument she had with her companion lasted longer than she cared for. Latros was a fearless soldier in the Voidwalker army. Being around so much death and living with the uncertainty of the possibility of never returning home made him demand she retire from her post. The frequency of this conversation was becoming too much for her to bear. She loved him, she really did, but she wished his overprotective and demanding ways would stop. As a result, she found herself storming out of his hut to go to her favorite place to clear her mind. When she remembered the meeting, she found herself nearly twenty minutes late.

"Nice of you to finally join us, Corporal," the Captain snapped.

"I apologize for my lateness ma'am, no excuse." Val replied.

Caitlin shook her head in disgust. "You better find your bearings and do it quickly. Now, sit."

She quickly took her seat at the end of the table. The council's hut was not the best hut in the Void. Its cold walls were lit by lanterns spaced at equal intervals. Everything about it was symmetrical. It was designed this way to always foster order. The large table in the middle was no different. This was Val's least favorite place. It lacked beauty and artistic flair, but she could not deny the reasoning for making this place in this fashion.

Glancing around the table, she noted that the Chief sat at the head of the table and next to him was Captain Caitlin. Directly across from her were Commanders Dia'tose, Shatrice, Mortaze, Gravelle, and Lunar followed by four Majors.

"Today we have received word the Valencians will hold their annual tournament two weeks from now. We have also received word that a new Second has been appointed among the enemy's commanders. Routen Ishtar."

Everyone immediately started hypothesizing what this meant. After several minutes, Caitlin slammed the table.

"You will mind your bearing."

Then, the Chief spoke. "This changes nothing. We will continue with our original plan. Plus, I believe there is more. Right, Corporal?"

Val cleared her throat. "Yes sir. I have received word through my networks that the girl we have been monitoring has begun to display abnormal traits."

"Abnormal?" Commander Dia'tose asked, raising an eyebrow.

"Yes. She took a fire attack head on without taking any damage."

The council looked at her in disbelief.

"Also, it seems during the last thunderstorm, it was reported she was struck by a massive bolt that seared her surroundings, but somehow she walked away without a scratch."

"Is she immune to the elements?" Commander Lunar asked.

She shrugged her shoulders. "My informant doesn't

know. They simply said it was strange, and they had not seen it before."

"So you're telling me this girl can deflect the elements and withstand being struck by lightning?" Lunar could not believe what he was hearing.

"I'm not sure. I have not been able to confirm any of these claims, also, they don't believe she is aware of these changes."

"Who is this girl?" Commander Gravelle asked. He spoke in a thick, rough tone as he drummed the table with his finger.

"She is a child stolen from her world," Caitlin answered. "Everything the Corporal has told you has also been confirmed by my informant."

"What world?" Commander Mortaze asked, crossing his arms.

"It seems that is a question with an elusive answer. It seems ten children from her world are here, and they all came at the same time. Apparently, they were taken from another trafficker before being brought here." Pressing forward, she rested her elbows on the table. "However, it appears there are at least two others in that House from their arrival." Caitlin said.

It had been long understood the Reinzour sought to conquer every world within the cosmos. When he learned of this world's ability to control the elements, he descended upon them like a hell storm. Though they fought, their war was over in the blink of an eye. The tactic of surprise left them all but defenseless as the invaders killed their leaders and arrested control of all they had. Immediately, they worked to extract the secrets of what the Inwatma people knew, but they quickly realized their power was one of compatibility. The colonizers, who referred to themselves as Valencians, prided themselves on research, and their ability to take other world's technology and make it theirs. However, this was not a product of technology, but appeared to be something passed through genetics. The first generation colonizers began capturing females of childbearing ages and funneled them through the sex trades. The Valencian men forced themselves on these women until they bore them children. This was the simplest solution to the compatibility issue. There was something about the people of this planet that allowed them to access this power.

As time passed, the Reinzour celebrated in the success of his endeavors. Though the Inwatma people fought back, they were no match for the collection of exotic traits the Valencians stole from other worlds. Realizing they could not overcome the challenges this war brought them, the Inwatma retreated to the area now referred to as the Void. As a result, the colonizers began referring to them as Voidwalkers. To protect their people, the men of a Yentosen Tribe surrendered their long life spans to use a power only known to them— time. Time magic is the rarest magic and required the life source of the wielder in return. The more they surrendered their life force, the stronger the effect. However, there was no life force great enough to end the invasion that had fallen upon them. Instead, the sacrifice of sixteen Yentosen created the barrier now protecting the Inwatma people. The Void Wall was constructed to replenish itself by draining the life force of any individual attempting to gain passage without permission. Since the Reinzour no longer had access to their women as breeders, he has been looking for a world of people, capable of wielding magic to enslave into his army. This was the real reason for the annual tournament and stolen children. If this child, and those like her, showed the ability to control the elements, every world was now at risk.

"And the barrier is starting to weaken," Caitlin said.

The weight of her words swallowed everyone to the depths of the sea and enveloped them under the pressure of the promise of hopelessness.

FORTY-FIVE

Confessions of the Heart

❝ Again! Your form is sloppy, and your movements are undisciplined," Narrock said.

After her match with Reynuck, Alli asked Narrock to instruct her. Right about now, she was regretting it. He had her follow his training regimen as he prepared for the tournament. Each day started with strength training that left her entire body soar. Before she had a chance to recover they were racing to the base of the mountain that the House of Ishtar sat atop and sprinting back uphill hauling stones twice their weight until he was satisfied. After a short break, it was a twenty-mile run at full speed. The pace was blistering, but she knew he had slowed his pace for her which was somewhat comforting. She did not allow herself to consider his true speed. When they had finished, there was no place she did not hurt, but training did not stop there. With body and mind throughly worked out, it was time to train the spirit through hours of rigorous sparring drills.

"I need a break," she gasped, trying to stop her lungs from seizing.

"You made it very clear that you didn't want to be treated as less than a warrior."

"I don't—"

"Then you get no sympathy from me." He turned away and continued his training.

After several moments of complaining and calling him out of his name under her breath, She got up and forced herself to continue. It had been nearly a month of training. First, at the Den and now with him, and she still could not land a single strike against him. It infuriated her. How had she managed to fall so far away from the foundation laid by Master Centrine?

"Enough."

He never had much to say during their training sessions unless he was admonishing her. She wiped the sweat from her brow with her towel and chugged some much-needed water. Just then, Ionis entered.

"I was starting to think you weren't going to make it," Alli said in greeting.

"Some of us still have responsibilities. Besides, cleaning the halls took a little longer than usual," she said.

Even though Ionis could not participate during the morning routine, she always found time to break away during the evening training sessions within the house.

"Ready?" His question was more of a command.

Alli and Ionis looked at each other and sighed deeply. They knew his response was not a question but a challenge. Together, they attacked.

He blocked everything. He called out their attacks before they made them. He told them where he would attack from, but they still could not defend against him. He deflected and rained down a steady barrage of attacks. They both found that their anger would frequently get the best of them.

"Master Centrine would be disappointed in both of you," he said as they lay on the floor panting like dogs. "Or have you forgotten all she has taught us?"

"No," Alli said.

"That is not what your training says."

Ionis scoffed. "Not everyone had the luxury of training every day. Some of us have to actually fight for our lives." She did not care that her words came out wrong.

"We're done," he said in a low whisper. Then he turned and left.

"Why would you say that?" Alli shouted.

"I didn't mean to! It's just, I'm so tired of him acting as if he is better than us."

"As a warrior, he is," Alli said, cutting her off.

"Look, he's not the only one who had a hard time with all of this! If he hasn't noticed."

Alli rubbed her temples with her middle fingers. "You know what your problem is? You act as if everyone owes you something."

"Don't talk to me about 'owing something,' *lady* Allister."

"What, you think I asked for this?"

"You did nothing to stop it. You're only lucky because Ishtar slept with you instead of me—". Before she registered what happened, Alli struck her across the face.

"Watch your damn mouth," she warned.

305

Wiping the blood from her mouth, Ionis stood. "You know what they say about you, right? That you're just his new plaything."

"I'm warning you. Shut up."

"Or what? Contrary to your belief, not everyone is willing to spread their legs for you."

The violence that ensued was destructive. Alli threw Ionis across the room. All the breath was knocked from her lungs as her body crashed into the wall. Furious, Ionis started hurling nearby objects at her. She dodged most of them, but a metal plate connected with a satisfying crack. Alli's balance wavered as blood flowed from the gash above her left eye. Before she could even wipe the blood from her face, Ionis was on top of her.

She quickly swept behind Alli and cinched her wrist around her waist. Alli had the strange sensation of floating until the extreme force of gravity hurled her towards the ground. The power of the suplex bounced her head against the stone floor. Her vision blinked in and out.

Both girls lay struggling for breath. Ionis was the first to her feet. In a rushed attempt, she launched her foot at her head. She may not have trained as much as Alli, but Ionis understood what to do when an enemy was weak. Alli dodged just in time and slammed her fist directly into her friend's esophagus before collapsing again.

Alli's senses were no longer in sync with one another, and after several minutes of gasping for air, Ionis' windpipe finally opened. Alli had trouble getting her body to cooperate with her thoughts. She felt the power of the kick that flipped her to her back. Her vision was again blurred, but this time, it was because of the pools of water now sitting atop both her eyes. She fought to regain focus as Ionis stood over her. Her eyes drifted along her sister's arm towards her hands. She could not fully make out what she was holding, but she knew. She watched as Ionis' lips flared, revealing two straight rows of teeth, before jamming a sword straight through her chest.

Her scream filled the room, clamoring to escape down the corridors as her mind snapped back into place. Ionis laughed hysterically. As she pulled the sword free from the sinew of her shoulder, blood dripping from the tip, she took a moment to plan her next strike. When she made up her mind, Ionis aimed the sword at Alli's throat. Placing both hands on the hilt of the sword, she put all her force in bringing it down on her friend with the intent of ending her life. Alli rolled to the side as the sword embedded itself into the floor, but when she turned back, not realizing that the sword was so close. Her own momentum sent her neck partway through the sword. She cried in agony.

"We were supposed to be in this together," tears making their way down her face. "Why did you leave me? Why did you forget about me?" Her face now rested in her hands as she sobbed uncontrollably.

Alli lay there trying to stop the bleeding. *Am I going to die?* Her final thought echoed as the light left her eyes.

FORTY-SIX

Next Stage

Narrock stormed out of the training hall at Ionis' insinuation. Yes, he was angry, but he had since moved beyond the place of turning that anger back on her. He understood she was hurting because she feels she had been left out, but he also knew they would have to discuss this later when his mind was capable of finding the right words.

He ventured to his favorite spot under the waterfall. Over the past month, he has found this was the best place to easily traverse to the Temple of Inderrah. Today was no exception. He took his usual spot and allowed the water to flow over his body. Closing his eyes, he stilled himself and ascended to meet Draxtin.

When he materialized on the mountaintop, he looked to Draxtin's regular resting place, but he was not there. He examined his surroundings and noticed nothing out of place. He cautiously approached Draxtin's boulder maintaining high alert. He was not sure what he was on alert for, but his understanding that he still felt pain in this plain spurred his caution. There was nothing. Unsure of what he should do, for some reason, he found himself moving toward the gate. Ever since he first arrived at this temple, the gate had always been open, but he only ever tried to enter the first day. Immediately, his eyes shot to the sky. The giant winged creature caught him by surprise the first time, but he would not allow it to toss him so easily this time. But he saw nothing monitoring the sky. When he reached the iron gates, he took a deep breath before placing his foot on the other side of the threshold.

A sense of disappointment weighed on him when nothing happened. For the first time, he noticed the temple was more of a ruin. Pillars lay broken across the courtyard. Webs of green vines grew across every surface and in every direction. Compared to the other two temples he had been too, this was by far the most unkempt. As he walked further, he saw what looked like grave markers. The warriors of

Jhatar had been taught to honor the sites of the fallen, so he did not stop to read them as he did not want to desecrate their resting place.

Carefully scouting his steps, he ambled over fallen debris and pushed aside low hanging vines. He could not help but wonder what this place looked like before it fell apart. After nearly an hour, he finally reached the stairs of the temple, and there at the base was another grave marker. As he read it from where he stood, the name Asher was carved into it. He froze.

"Asher was not from Jhatar. Why is his grave here?" he asked out loud.

"It's simple, Do you know what the Temple of Inderrah is?" Draxtin asked, appearing at the top of the steps.

"It is where we come to release our spiritual limit."

"I did not ask why you came here. I asked you what it is."

Narrock was at a loss for words. He had been coming to this place hoping to unlock his spiritual upper limit, but never once did he consider what this place truly was.

"There are grave markers," he said after a while. "That means this Temple is a resting place for the souls of our people."

His ancestor shook his head. "How many of the graves did you visit?"

"Only this one," he replied,

"Why?"

"I am not prepared to tend to these graves without desecrating them."

"Stupid boy, you are in the temple of the soul. How would you desecrate the dead here?" Draxtin laughed.

Faster than he could blink, he found himself again standing at the gates of the temple. This time when he entered, Draxtin's words echoed through his thoughts. As he moved forward, he stopped to visit each grave. The first grave had the name Torrock inscribed on it. He felt as if he swallowed a large rock. Torrock was the name of his elder brother. Instantly he was transported back in time to relive the painful memories of his past. When he was younger, he developed a level of admiration for his brother unlike any he had for anyone other than his father. His brother was everything he wanted to be. He trained hard with him, but as he grew older, his brother became distant. Holding in tears threating to flood the temple, he was confronted by memories he purposely forgot. Memory after memory of his brother played, one after the other, until they reached his last memory of him. Torrock was preparing to leave for a mission on which he would be gone for an extended period. Narrock watched as his brother took his younger self into the woods to train. He listened as his brother explained he would be gone for a while.

"When I come back, I promise I will spend more time with you." The words from his brother strangled his heart.

Without thinking, he yelled, "Don't go Torrock!" and stretched his hand out toward him.

Torrock could not hear him because this was only a memory. His brother would die on the same day he left out. He watched as he stood by his brother's side in the healing halls.

"I hate you. You lied to me, and I hate you."

His brother's face was full of tears as his spirit left his body. Narrock broke. He had been so selfish and childish at that moment. He had forgotten about his brother after he placed his mission over him. He had not realized the ethos of a warrior at that time, but now he understood them well.

He again found himself standing before Torrock's grave. He wiped his face and moved on to the next. When he found himself standing before Asher's grave again, he no longer questioned why it was here. He recalled the final moments of the fighter's life as he stood by idly watching while the Reinzour murdered him on the auction block.

"Have you realized what this place is?" Draxtin asked for the second time.

"It is my soul,"

Filled with shame and remorse, his heart felt ready to burst.

Nodding. "What have you learned, young warrior?"

He opened his mouth to speak but was quickly cut off by his ancestor.

"A warrior does not bow their head."

"I have learned of the bitterness in my heart against others."

"Is this all you have learned?"

He noted how Draxtin eyed him curiously as he continued.

"No. I have judged many through a tainted lens of self-exhortation. I held them accountable for failing me when they did their best to protect me." Tears fell onto his cheeks. "I have beared grudges against people who have loved me and that I was too stubborn to see."

"I see," Draxtin said as he descended the steps. "And

have you forgiven those of whom you speak?"

"Yes." He tried to wipe the tears from his face, but they were falling faster than he realized.

"And what of yourself, what have you seen?"

He tried to clear the lump in his throat, "I have realized the one who has truly failed in my life is me. I never wanted to accept my part in any of these issues because it was easier to blame everyone else." His voice cracked as he spoke, looking away from his ancestor.

"A warrior never looks away."

Taking a deep breath, "I should have been a better son. A better brother. And a better friend. But I wasn't. I discarded people and expected everyone to bow to me. I warped reality to fit my perspective, and I took my frustration out on everybody else instead of holding myself accountable."

"I see. And have you forgiven yourself?"

A long moment passed before he spoke. "I don't know how."

Burying his face in his hands, he sobbed. Draxtin pulled the young warrior into his embrace. They stayed like that for several moments before he held him at arm's length.

"To forgive yourself is no different than forgiving

others." Draxtin said, aware his words sounded easier to speak than to actually do. "We all make mistakes; the key is gaining insight from our mistakes and growing from them. Now, I will ask you again, have you forgiven yourself?" Releasing him, he took a step back.

Narrock wiped the tears and snot from his face. Standing tall, he opened his eyes and answered.

"Yes."

Draxtin smiled and gestured for him to turn around. When he did, the temple courtyard was no longer in ruin, but had been returned to a state of complete restoration. As he turned back to Draxtin, the stone doors to the temple opened.

FORTY-SEVEN

Chains Broken

Alli awoke in the healing halls. The room was dimly lit and had a particular smell to it that made her eyes flutter. As she tried to sit up fire coursed from both her shoulder and her neck. Taking her right hand, she gingerly explored the areas causing her pain. As she felt over her shoulder, tears began to form, and when she reached her neck, they fell without constraint. The bandage wrapping her body was wet in only two places, and as she touched the blood-soaked clothes, everything came back.

Why had Ionis tried to kill her? They were like sisters, and today, she treated her like an enemy. *Why did you leave me? Why did you forget about me?* Ionis' words echoed through her thoughts. Had she left her? Had she forgotten? There was no way she had done such a cruel thing. Sure, she did not have the same time for her, and of course she had been named a lady of Ishtar's House, but certainly that did not equate to her leaving Ionis behind, did it?

This back and forth introspection continued until her thoughts were shattered by a knock at the door. The hinges moaned as the door scratched across the floor. She only moved her eyes, not wanting to experience the sensation of fire burning through her body again, to see Ishtar enter. She listened intently to the hollow thud of his steps as he approached, the clank of the stool he placed next to her, the muffled thump of his body hitting the seat, and then she felt the warmth of his touch as he slipped his hand into hers.

"Are you alright," he asked.

His voice was like a calming stream. She managed to let out a shaky yes, and they sat there for several minutes without saying anything.

"Where is she?" Despite the pain, she turned so her eyes met his gaze.

He averted his eyes and said nothing for a few minutes

before turning back.

"She is in a holding cell."

"Please do not hurt her."

"Why should you care? She tried to kill you," his grip tightening around her fingers.

"Because, she is my sister, and sisters fight."

She forced a smile on her face that did not match the truth in her heart. Gone was the love she had for Ionis and in its place was pure unadulterated hate. In earnest, the only reason she advocated for her life was out of respect for Narrock.

"And I'm supposed to just accept that answer?" He stood violently. The stool clanged against the floor.

She looked away, "As far as I know, we are the last of our people here. I can't be the reason one of us dies," her words choked.

"This is the third time I have failed to protect you in this house."

He slammed his fist on the wall before resting his head upon it. After a long pause, without looking back, he asked.

"Why have you been avoiding me?"

Alli knew she would not be able to elude him. Ever

since they returned from the auction and she had to share a chamber with him, she had done her best to avoid him. Instead of sharing the room with him, she would stay with Erridus or Ionis. When they were in public together, she was fine, but whenever he attempted to seclude her to talk, she always found a way to escape.

"I'm sorry, but I think I need to rest."

"Bull-shit!" Ishtar flung around to meet her gaze.

She was stunned. In all the time she had been in this house, she never heard Ishtar use such vulgar words. As far as she knew, he abhorred such words and did not tolerate the use of them in his presence.

"This is exactly what I'm talking about. What have I done to make you hate me?"

His words like needles throughout her heart. Even though she knew she should not have, she forced herself to sit up.

"Is that what you think?"

"You tell me! What am I supposed to think when you won't even speak to me?" his voice cracked.

Her hand felt like stone as she started to reach for him and stopped.

"I don't hate you," she said softly

"Then what is it?" he asked, moving closer.

"I, I don't know," she turned and looked down to her hand as they gripped the sheets.

"I will not accept that as an answer. Is it because I've made you share my chamber? Is it because I made you a lady? Or is it because you are in love with Narrock?!"

"No!" she said much more forcefully then she intended.

"Oh, come on. I see the way you look at him. How long do you expect me to buy the 'he's my brother' crap?"

"How dare you. You don't have the right to infer anything about me. Not Narrock, not Ionis, and especially not you."

"I didn't mean it like that—"

"Yes, you did! I am tired of everybody assuming that I'm just sleeping with everybody. And the fact that you would think I would sleep with someone else when I'm in love with you—" she clasped her hands around her mouth as if the last part of what she said would have been snuffed out.

Ishtar's eyes open wide. "You what?" All of his attention focused on her.

"Nothing, I said nothing. It's the medicine. It makes

me say things I'm not sure of."

She knew this sounded ridiculous, but she was not sure of what else to say. She watched him pick up the stool and returned it to its place. Then he started to the door.

"You know, you are not the only one who is unsure of what to do with their feelings. When you are ready, maybe we can share the secrets of our hearts, together." He grabbed the handle of the door to leave.

"Wait," she said, reaching for him. "About Ionis—"

"Don't worry, it's not me she will answer to. It's Narrock." He pulled the door open and stepped through.

"Ishtar?" He paused. "About sharing. One day, I would very much like that."

"I'd like that too." He turned his head and smiled, then pulled the door shut behind him.

It had been four days since her fight with Ionis. The healers finished working on her yesterday, but at Ishtar's insistence, they held her in the infirmary for an extra day. Alli looked outside her window and noticed the sky. It was full of fury, which was precisely how she felt right now. She could not believe Ionis, her kindred, attempted to kill her. The way Narrock handled it gave her no pleasure either. He simply forced her to train until she could not move. She let out a low snarl. She wanted him to have at least beat her senseless, but she knew better than anyone that his warrior spirit and sense of protection would not allow him.

She found it strange when she thought about how Narrock acted just like the masters from Jhatar. Shoving the thought from her mind, she was determined to blow off some steam. As she was putting on her fighting clothes, Erridus let herself in.

"So, the first thing you do when you get released is prepare to crack skulls?"

Alli laughed, "She is my sister."

"Listen, Allister—"

"Call me Alli."

Erridus paused as if trying to find the right words.

"Alli, for what it's worth, I'm sorry. I know it hasn't been easy, and it probably might get worse in the near future, but I hope you would see me as your kindred too."

She was not used to seeing her fidget the way she was. She had always been so confident and sure of herself that she was often envious of her. Crossing the room, she took Erridus' hands in hers.

"Of course." The two shared a knowing smile, "Even though you kidnapped me and threw me in a ring to get beat unconscious."

Erridus feigned a baffled expression and she gasped as if offended. The melody of laughter filled the room.

"But seriously, Alli," her face returned to the somber expression she wore on her way in. "We have always tried to protect you. And know, I will continue to protect you." She pulled her in for a strong embrace before slipping out her room.

She was not sure how to take what just happened, but when she glanced out of her window, she could hear her souls cry for retribution.

Since Narrock returned from Inderrah, he had been hearing a strange voice in his head calling for him. He was not sure why, but one thing was for sure, he completed the initial stage of his journey to release his spiritual limits. He hoped he would be able to use his hardening ability once more but quickly discovered he had not completed the entire release.

He found himself wondering how he would win this tournament without it. For him, hardening had been the one thing that protected him the most during his time in the Coliseum. He began to recount the many times he would have surely died without it but also reminded himself he was still a young warrior. In the ten years since he had been here, he honed his body and mind into a true warrior. Or so he thought. Draxtin had shown him that his lack of care for his soul was holding him back from truly becoming a warrior.

Where are you?

He shook his head as if he could dispel the growling voice from his head. His mind returned to trying to understand why Draxtin ordered he not return to Inderrah until five days passed. He wanted to go back to see if his ancestor knew what was going on, but despite his want to know, he knew he needed to obey. So instead, he asked Ishtar to place Ionis under his care. He could not believe what she had done after he left that day, but he also understood she had been suffering.

For three days he forced her to meditate. He trained her mind and body and made sure at the end of the day she took time to restore her spirit. This did not stop her from whining from sun up to sun down. Today was no different.

"Why don't you just go ahead and save both of us the time and kill me now?"

He was beginning to lose patience with her whining.

"Because that is a death you are undeserving of. Now pick up the pace."

She closed her mouth and quickened her pace. Something in his eyes matched the terror hanging in the clouds, and she did not want that unleashed on her.

Where are you?

Stopping, his eyes darted in every direction and he extended his perception as far as it would reach. As usual, he felt nothing.

"Did you hear anything just now?"

Ionis dropped the sack twice her weight and hunched over, her hands on her knees, panting.

"Hear what?"

He surveyed the land once more before his gaze returned to her.

"Did I say you could drop your pack?"

She scrambled to pick it back up and, for once, decided to keep her mouth shut.

Alli stormed down the hallway praying she would not run into Ionis. She was pretty sure she would not be able to contain her rage if she did. As if she was being tempted she cursed under her breath as Reynuck headed straight for her.

"Ah, lady Allister," he said, executing a mocking bow.

"Piss off, Reynuck."

"Why, that is not the proper language of a lady. Besides, I just wanted to tell you how happy I am to see you are doing well." Leaning in, he whispered so only she could hear him, "Given that your ass was handed to you," he snickered. "So tell me, bitch, how does it feel?" He peeled back, a joker's smile painted on his face. "Do try to be more careful," he said as he continued down the corridor.

The sound of thunder cracking returned her from her murderous thoughts. "I swear I wish someone would kill him already."

As Alli approached the Den, she was greeted by K'La.

"Unless you're here to meet me in the cage, I have nothing to say to you," she shouted.

K'La lifted both her hands, palms out, a sign that she meant her no harm.

"I'm not here to fight you."

"Then what do you want?"

"Look, I came to give you some advice."

Alli did not wait for her to finish. She pushed past K'La and entered the Den. She watched until the bout ended and before the announcer could ask for the next challenger, she had already stepped into the cage and slammed it shut.

"So tiny," the fighter said.

Alli said nothing. Instead, she allowed all the rage that had built up to completely absorb her. Red tinted her eyes as her mind snapped into focus.

"Ladies and gentlemen, please place your bets."

She did not hear the crowd shouting her name, nor did she hear the announcer. She locked onto her target and was only waiting to hear the bell. Her opponent was nicknamed the She-Devil. She was a brutal fighter. Several times she violated the rules regarding killing an opponent, but she was never banned because of the vast amount of revenue her bouts generated. She had never been defeated, and her opponents have never left the cage without at least one broken bone.

When the bell finally sounded, Alli pounced. She unleashed a volley of punches into the She-Devil's guard. She connected with a wild left, followed by a devastating uppercut. This sent the fighter reeling back. Before she could gather herself, she charged, not wanting to give her opponent a second to breathe. Again, she unleashed several attacks like the flapping of hummingbird's wings. She was unstoppable—until the She-Devil connected a solid shot to her rib cage. *Crack*! It felt as if a nest of angry hornets were set loose along her nervous system. The massive barbarian was quicker on her feet than she realized. No sooner than her punch connected was she behind her, arms locked around her waist. In one fluid motion, Alli was lifted off her feet and buried into the ground. Landing on the base of her neck, the red in her eyes wavered, replaced by blue as tears were knocked loose.

Clearing her thoughts, she quickly stood, taking a fighter's stance. The She-Devil smiled. Alli roared as she charged again. Her opponent threw a blazing haymaker, but she ducked under it and leapt from her planted foot. Interlocking her fist together, she brought them down hard across the back of the fighter's head while simultaneously bringing her knee through her chin. The She-Devil screamed in pain. The force of her attacks caused her opponent to bite through her tongue. She watched as the brutish female reached up and ripped the hanging piece away. The laugh that slithered out of her mouth was demonic. Wiping her meaty arm across her mouth, the She-Devil spat a pool of blood onto the ground and instantly had Alli by the throat. She rocketed her toward the sky with one hand and slammed her through the floor of the Den. In one smooth motion, all the air had been snatched from her body.

"This one has fight," she said as she hovered her face over hers.

Alli had to hold back the vomit rising as the She-Devil's blood splattered across her face and in her mouth. All at once, she gathered in as much strength as she could muster before launching her fist directly into the fighter's windpipe. The She-Devil collapsed to the ground clawing her throat.

The crowd erupted in cheers. The Den was so loud no one noticed the droplets of rain beating upon the earth like drums signaling war. It was Alli who stood to her feet first. She stood bent over, hands on her knees, and vomited the blood she swallowed. Again, red tainted her vision. As the She-Devil attempted to push herself up, one knee on the ground the other leg bent, Alli pivoted on her forward leg and hurled a thunderous kick across the side of the fighter's face. The force of her blow dislodged several teeth from her opponent's mouth. The giant female made her way to her feet. She stuck what remained of her tongue through the gaps in her teeth and smiled.

For a moment, Alli stood in shock. This monster's tolerance of pain was unnerving. Not wasting any more time, she darted right for her. Before she realized, the massive female crouched down and fired a debilitating punch through her torso. Alli was launched off her feet and found herself looking the She-Devil in the eyes. As she began her descent to the ground, she felt hands clasp around the back of her head, hurling her downward. It was all she could do to bring her hands in front of her face to deflect the power of the She-Devil's upward thrusting knee. What was red was now black. When her vision returned, she felt the pressure of the fighter's foot on her abdomen. She blinked feverishly, trying to absolve the dancing dots impairing her sight.

"Tiny girl wants more," she said as she reached down to grip her by the throat.

As she lifted her off her feet, she flashed her decimated smile. Alli pulled back both her hands and slammed them across the fighter's ears. The She-Devil dropped her and held her ears. Blood leaked from her ruptured eardrums. This time, the She-Devil did not smile. She looked as if she had been possessed. She stalked over to Alli, but Alli did not wait. She plunged the base of her palm into her nose. Blood gushed as she fell backward, landing on the ground. Alli quickly mounted her and began raining down hammer fists.

She beat her head in cadence with the rain. She pounded until she felt bone give. She stood, exhausted, and stumbled backward. Thinking the fight was over, she exhaled a deep breath and started for the exit. The massive fighter raised her head and turned to her side. She forced herself to stand.

"Now, you die!" she said.

For whatever reason, Alli found herself in the training hall with Ionis again. She looked up as Ionis drove down the sword, and something in her snapped. She screamed. The She-Devil stopped in her tracks as Alli's hair began to stand on itself. Tendrils of bluish purple sparks flickered across her fingers. The ground started to shake until it split open, and the canvas of the Den was cleaved. As everyone looked in horror, the brilliant blaze of a dragon made of lightning shot straight down and incinerated the She-Devil where she stood.

She stood in disbelief. What had she just done? Before she knew it, her body reacted. Her feet ran, and her unresponsive mind just followed. When she finally stopped, she fought desperately to break through the illusion cast upon her mind. *I didn't. I couldn't have.* Her thoughts were a mess of emotions and visions, none of which she could decipher at the moment. Tears fell from her eyes. Then, her world was engulfed in darkness. Flailing in every direction, she could not make sense why everything suddenly disappeared.

"Who's there?" she cried, but no one answered.

Thwack!

It had been late in the evening when Ishtar summoned Narrock.

"You know, this used to be my personal haven. Now it seems like everyone knows about it." He made a gesture towards the waterfall.

"Is there a reason you brought me here?"

"Yes."

Ishtar paused. He had not always been able to get along with the male in front of him. In truth, Narrock's unbreakable will and warrior spirit are what made this all the more difficult.

"Well?" Narrock asked.

"You see, something has happened to Allister." Fire danced in Narrock's eyes. Noticing, Ishtar lifted his hands. "We are not sure, but it seems she has been kidnapped."

"I knew I should not have trusted you," Narrock growled, pointing an accusatory finger.

"It seems that there was a shaking of the earth and a lightning storm in town today." He could tell his explanation was doing nothing to improve the situation. "No one is sure what happened, but when my men followed the direction she left in, the only thing they found was this." Ishtar held up the leather band.

Narrock recognized it immediately. Master Centrine had given all her students a band when they studied with her. Etched equal spaces apart were the symbols for the tenant of physical release.

"I'm sorry, we—" he stopped as he noticed the air around Narrock looked as if it was melting. "It can't be."

Even though the rain ended, the ground still bore evidence of its recent passing. Yet, where Narrock stood was bone dry. Ishtar could no longer make out Narrock's features. Instead, standing before him was his silhouette accented by flames where his eyes should be. For every step he took, Ishtar found his smile growing in excitement until laughter was dancing from his mouth.

Narrock had been engulfed in flames. His flames burned brighter than any dragon-spawned he knew. The flames spread as they licked up every ounce of moisture in the area. The pool began to boil, and every breath Ishtar took burned. Narrock stopped ten paces from Ishtar and suddenly looked over to the cave entrance.

There you are. He knew this voice, for stalking out from the mouth of the cave was the Lokia that nearly killed him. *You are not ready for these flames yet.*

Then, in an instant, his flames were snuffed out. The Lokia continued in the direction of Narrock before taking a seat between the two males.

"This changes everything." Ishtar stared at Narrock in delight.

As color slowly returned to Alli's vision, she was keenly aware she was no longer in the city. Sitting up, she looked around the small hut and tried to make sense of what happened. As she thought about everything leading up to this point, tears began to slide across her face. She killed that fighter. She tried to rationalize with herself. *No one from my world can control the skies.* Yet she did.

Not only that, but she also made the ground break. A memory flashed into her thoughts. The dragon in her dream, the dragon that split the sky, and the dragon that killed the She-Devil, they were the same. Just then, the flap to her hut opened and in walked two women.

"Where am I?" she asked.

Although, she did not expect to have her questions

answered. She had heard enough of how prisoners were usually treated from her time schmoozing the Toultyn as a servant.

The female clad in black armor answered.

"Why, you are in the Void."

Author's Note

Life is precious. In fact, it is the most precious thing on this Earth. As a brown-skinned American, it saddens me that my children are growing up in a society that is still facing the civil rights issues my parents and grandparents faced in the 60s. Society today praises Dr. Martin Luther King Jr.'s *I have A Dream* speech; yet, in truth does not honor that speech in their actions. Brown- and black-skinned Americans lives are devalued based on the color of our skin. I have heard the conversation said, "If he didn't look like a thug," or, "if he would have just listened," or, "black lives need to matter first to black people," and countless other statements when it comes to the death of an unarmed Brown-skinned American, and the truth is that it should not matter. It should not matter what an individual looks like, their educational background, the neighborhood they grow-up in, or the social-economical class they belong to. Thomas Jefferson wrote in The

Declaration of Independence the following, "We hold these truths to be self-evident, that all men are created equal, that they are endowed by their Creator with certain unalienable Rights, that among these are Life, Liberty and the pursuit of Happiness." If life is the most precious thing on this Earth, then we need to act now to protect it. It does not matter what your ethnicity is, or what your political affiliation is. What matters is the legacy we leave to our children. My son is six months old and as an American citizen, I should not have to shed tears over the fact that my son's life could be cut short simply because of the color of his skin. Black Lives Matter is not a statement that takes away from the importance of any other ethnicity. It is, however, an affirmation that we are included when Thomas Jefferson wrote "that they are endowed by their Creator with certain unalienable Rights." Now is the time to take Dr. King's dream, and make it a reality. Now is the time to ensure that every ethnicities' rights to life, liberty and the pursuit of happiness is protected. Now is the time to end police brutality and social injustice. Now is the time to create an America where black families no longer have to fight with others to get them to understand that BLACK LIVES MATTER TOO. Now is the time to create a society where no other ethnicity has to say that because we will be a society that honors the unalienable rights granted to all men and women by the Creator.

If you have enjoyed book one of the The Upper Limits: Unbreakable, please consider leaving a comment on Amazon,

Goodreads, or my website www.Creativemyownway.com. In addition, if you sign up for my newsletter, you will be among the first to get sneak peaks in to my upcoming projects, and may even be selected to pre-screen and provide inputs for selections.

Thank you again for reading Unbreakable. If you would like to follow me on social media, you can follow me on instagram @creative_my_own_way.

CPSIA information can be obtained
at www.ICGtesting.com
Printed in the USA
LVHW091531211020
669425LV00024B/598/J